Psychic Widow

Karen Canavan

13/11/2016

To Meena
with love
Karen x

Published by New Generation Publishing in 2016

Copyright © Karen Canavan 2016

First Edition

ISBN 978-1-78507-888-0

www.newgeneration-publishing.com

About the Author

Karen has been married to her husband, Stephen for sixteen years, and together they have two children. She works part-time within a nursery during the day and provides psychic readings by night. She achieved her Reiki Master Degree, which she uses to help people. After reading various romance novels over the years, she felt that it was time for her to put pen to paper.

I dedicate the writing of Psychic Widow to my dad, Paul Thomas Henshaw, who passed away on 20th May 2015. Thanks for all the good times and for the last holiday spent together at Norfolk Broads, memories of which I will treasure until I join you in the next life.

Love you loads, your little girl x

Chapter One

I sit at my desk in my office feeling bored after just finishing yet another boring telephone conversation. *When will something exciting happen in my life?* I wonder, as I look out of the window into the busy street outside. These boring injury claims are all the same – "this car went into that" – the same old compensation claims. I need more excitement in my life and wonder *where can I take Grace this evening?* She has been so distant lately, I'm beginning to wonder if being engaged to her is the right thing for my future.

The phone rings distracting me from my thoughts: "Russell Edwards." I answer with the same enthusiasm as my current mood *what is wrong with me today.*

"Mr Edwards, I have your sister Rosanna on the phone for you. Shall I put her through?"

"Yes, Mrs Jones. Oh and a coffee wouldn't go a miss, thank you." Mrs Jones, a dear sweet personal assistant of mine. I have known her for almost five years now, and always willing to lend a hand.

"Of course, Mr Edwards."

What does Rosanna want? She doesn't usually ring me at the office.

"Hello, Rosanna, is everything alright?"

"Hi, Russell, yeah everything's fine. Just ringing to ask what you and Grace are up to this evening? Only I'm going to a show in London. Jean and Michelle were coming with me but Jean's gone down with the flu and Michelle needs to go and see her grandma, as she was taken ill this morning."

"Nothing too serious I hope?"

"Not sure yet, I'll let you know later. So, anyhow… what about this show? I have two tickets going and don't want to go on my own."

"Oh it's not one of those mumbo jumbo weirdo shows you're always going to, is it?"

1

"They are not 'Mumbo Jumbo', besides, Grace found it fascinating last time she came with me."

"Who are you seeing this time, 'Nelly the Elephant', and how much of a rip off were the tickets. You do know it's just all a money making scam, don't you? It's all a set-up. When has anyone ever come to you?" *But I suppose Grace did enjoy going last time*, I think to myself, *even though I'd probably be bored all evening.*

"For your information, Russell, this is a charity evening, and all proceedings go to the MacMillan Nurses. This medium only does shows for charity. Mystic Pen and guest Rose, who occasionally work together on stage, only work for charity. Please say you'll come, I've never seen them before and I really can't go on my own."

"I'll have to check with Grace then get back to you, but I suppose if it's for charity, I'll be bored out of my brains all evening though." I can't believe I just said that, am I really going to go to one of those shows my sister's always going on about. She's so desperate for answers to Suzie's death she'll believe anything. As much as it pains me to think it, Suzie starved herself to death and has gone, that's it…nothing more to say on the subject, although just the thought of not being able to help brings a lump to my throat.

"Great, the show starts at 7.30pm. Shall I meet you at the entrance at 7.00pm?"

"Supposing we are going, I'll see if I can arrange for Gibson to pick you up and we'll all go together."

Typical of my brother always wanting to make sure I get there in one piece. "OK, what time?" "About 5.30pm."

"That's settled then, see you at 5.30pm and, Russell, thanks."

And before I can answer she's gone, just like Rosanna. Great, now my evening is going to be as boring as my day. I sigh as Mrs Jones brings my coffee and biscuits in.

"Thought the biscuits might cheer you up, Mr Edwards," says Mrs Jones.

I very much doubt that, but the thought is nice. "Thank

you, Mrs Jones, everything's fine. Just been conned into going to one of those shows with Rosanna."

"I'm sure you'll have a pleasant evening, Mr Edwards. You know Rosanna just needs a sign then she will be able to grieve properly."

"Um" is all I manage to say. Mrs Jones doesn't usually comment on such things and what possible sign could Rosanna be given? Suzie's gone and that's it, and we did absolutely nothing to help. I feel that lump form in my throat again. I must get on with these reports to see who's at fault. That should take my mind of Suzie, and Grace for that matter.

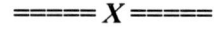

Chapter Two

We arrive at the theatre at 7.10pm. Grace has been on the phone texting on and off the whole journey. *What is she up to?* I wonder. As we enter the West End Theatre, the place is spectacular. Having seen various shows here over the years, I am always in awe of these magnificent theatres. It's just a shame that this show will be one without excitement…but wait a minute, is that a picture of the medium on stage tonight.

Her piercing blue eyes and long black velvet hair, maybe it was worth coming just for the view. She is certainly stunning, and there is something familiar about those eyes, so cold yet compassionate all at the same time. It feels like I know her somehow, but I can't for the life of me think how.

Rosanna interrupts my thoughts. "Come on, Russell, we need to find our seats. I've arranged for us to sit in the centre stalls at the back. Sorry, I know you prefer a private box but you know I can't do heights."

"OK, shall we get some refreshments?"

"Nothing for me thanks."

"Grace, would you like anything?"

"Um, what, oh, no thanks, I'll wait till the interval."

I look over at the queue and think, *well maybe I'll wait then.*

There's a knock on my dressing room door. "Come in," I call.

"Hi, Pen, are you nearly ready? We're due on stage in ten minutes."

"Yes, almost done Rose." Rose has been such a dear friend to me over the years, and although she is many years older than myself, she doesn't act it. I remember with great appreciation all the difficult times she has helped me through in my life, and I certainly couldn't have developed my mediumship without her, and for that I'm eternally grateful.

I rise from my vanity seat after applying my lipstick and give my old friend a quick squeeze saying, "its show time. After you."

We make our way to the stage door and I can feel the usual butterflies in my stomach. In front of us, I can sense and feel Soul's presence. Soul my beautiful, strong warrior guide, who's always there for me. Loving and protecting me throughout my whole life without judgement, it is such an honour to work for these higher beings of light. If only everyone knew and understood what help they could receive from these higher beings.

The stage door opens and we're on; as soon as I step onto the stage I see an elderly gentleman, who seems to be waiting impatiently. Then further away from him, I see a rather gaunt looking girl; she's very timid, almost afraid to be here. I give her a reassuring smile and say to her in my mind, *this is your first time, it's OK, and there is nothing here that can harm you now.* We only work with love and light. She gives me a smile in return for my reassurance.

"Good evening, ladies and gentleman, and welcome to Mystic Pen's Clairvoyant evening. I have a special guest with me this evening. Mrs Rose Hyde, who has kindly agreed to join me here on stage. To those of you who haven't been to one of my shows before, it's quite simple. I just describe the loved one that I have here on stage with me and find the person within the audience they wish to pass a message on to. I will do my best to deliver the correct message and answer any questions you may have for them. All I ask from yourselves is a simple Yes or No answer, so that I know I'm giving the right messages to the right person.

"For those of you that are sitting there thinking, 'I'm not sure if this is real?' Well, I'm not here to convince you either way. I just ask that you except the messages and love from your loved ones in the spirit world, then decide for yourself.

5

"Now, there is a lot of you in the audience here this evening; between Rose and myself, we will do our best to get the messages through to as many in the audience as possible. I usually find at these big events, that the way in which spirits work is they usually find the people that are most in need of comfort at this particular time. Now, that doesn't mean your loved ones are not here for you all; remember, they are only a thought away.

"When I walked on to this stage there was an elderly gentleman standing right over there." I point to the right side of the stage. "He wants to talk to Doreen, and he is very impatient."

I look up and find the light which leads the way. It takes me to the right hand side of the theatre, and right at the top I see a grey-haired lady and I meet her eyes.

"Eugene, can you please move the light and mic to the lady sitting in the top right hand row, thank you. Doreen, my dear, is your husband Alfred in spirit?"

From the minute she walks on stage I'm hooked. Wow she is stunning, short black skirt, revealing her long tanned legs, and low cut top, leaving little to the imagination. God, it's enough to make a man twitch in areas that it shouldn't in these environments (down boy). She must be about five-foot eight inches tall in those stiletto shoes and her piercing blue eyes…well, they just have so much focus and compassion for the lady she's talking to. I mustn't let myself be fooled by good looks as it's probably just all a big set up.

Then she looks up and her eyes lock with mine. I'm sure I've met her before, it feels like I know her somehow. *But how? And what does she want with me anyway?*

"Russell, I have your sister here on stage with me. Is there someone with you? Good, your other sister is here, next to you? Would you mind standing together for support? I know it can be a little intimidating standing on your own in front of all these people."

As I lock eyes with this man, I feel like I know him somehow. It throw's me slightly, only slightly, but he is so good looking and those eyes are just gorgeous.

"Russell, or should I say Russ, as your sister Suzie would call you. She's the only one that could call you this, she tells me. Is that correct?"

OK, now I'm intrigued, no one could possible know that. I hate the name Russ, and only Suzie ever called me Russ.

"Yes, that's correct. She is the only one who ever called me Russ."

"That's because you don't really like being called Russ, is what she tells me. She also tells me that you feel guilty for not helping her? Is this true?"

"Yes, that's true. We all should have done more."

"Well I can tell you now that she doesn't want you to feel guilty any longer. She says there is nothing whatsoever anyone of you could have done or said. Every time she looked in the mirror she felt fat. It didn't matter how many times any of you told her she was beautiful and slim, she always felt ugly and overweight. By the time she realised that what you all were saying was true, it was simply too late. Her body couldn't take any more; it had become far too weak and her heart just gave way in the end. Does this make sense to you? There is no other easy way of saying it."

"Yes, perfect sense."

"She also wants me to say, she is concerned for you at this moment in time. The company you're keeping is not being true to you. She says, that you know something is wrong but you are not sure what, and this is one of the reasons she's here tonight, to look out for you."

As she gives me this message her eyes lock with Grace's and go cold. What is she trying to say? I wonder? I know things are not right…that much is true.

"I'll leave her love with you and leave you with one thought, two's a partnership, and three's a crowd. God

Bless, I hope it all works out for you."

"OK, thank you." *I think.*

The rest of the evening passes in much the same way. Pen and Rose taking it in turns to speak to people within the audience giving various messages. I'm not quite sure I really follow anything else about the evening. I'm curious as to the message that has been given to me and the beauty of the lady that has given me the message. I must find out more about her, and how did she know some of the things that are personal to me?

"I would like to thank you all for joining Rose and myself here in London this evening. Please take with you what you can from this experience. Accept the love that has been given to you from your loved ones in the spirit world; heaven is not a million miles away, just a mere thought of a loved one brings them to your side

"I would just like to leave you with one thought: 'Earth has no sorrow that heaven cannot heal'. Goodnight, God bless to you all and have a safe journey home."

With that she blows a kiss to the audience and walks calmly off the stage.

As we walk back to our dressing rooms Rose turns to me, "What was that between you and that guy in the audience?"

"I don't know what you mean, Rose?" I say, playing the innocent.

"That guy, I saw the way he looked at you and the way in which you looked at him. You know he's your soul mate, don't you?"

'She's right there, he is your soul mate,' Soul whispers in my ear. *Oh, don't you start,* I think to myself.

"Yeah, right. You know I'm done with men, Rose. William was enough to last me a lifetime."

But there was something very familiar about him that I just can't put my finger on, and he was hot, really hot in fact.

"Have it your way," Rose says. "But I'm telling you, there is chemistry between you. Watch this space."

"Yeah, right."

===== *X* =====

Chapter Three

I make my way up the steps of the Tate Gallery after spending most of the morning researching some history on Mystic Pen, who turns out to be Penelope West a famous artist. I can't get this woman out of my head. The things she said last night keep playing on my mind. No one could have known any of that personal information, even if she had researched my information. There is just no way she could have known that Suzie called me Russ, which, yes I hate the name Russ, only let Suzie get away with it because she was ill.

I'm hoping my visit here today will settle my curiosity; you never know, I might even bump into her. I'm secretly hoping so; she was certainly one of the most beautiful women I've ever seen. Those eyes were so familiar; I feel I know her somehow, but I can't think for the life of me how?

As I walk inside the doors there is a sculpture of some kind in the centre of the entrance. I can't believe I've never been inside this magnificent building before. High ceilings, very grand and beautiful...a bit like her. God, I can't stop thinking about her and it does something to me, that I know for sure.

After collecting the various information leaflets, I absentmindedly look at the map, not concentrating at all on what I'm looking at. I make my way to one of the exhibition rooms when, ah, what, I'm falling backwards. Oh, how embarrassing, I'm going to fall flat on my arse in front of all these people. Only, before I know it I'm being caught by someone. Um, they sure smell nice, I've been caught by someone with expensive taste in perfume. A woman, how embarrassing, honestly.

"Russell, isn't it? Are you alright? Come take a seat over here.

"Who is responsible for cleaning up around here,

something has been spilt on the floor down there. You over there, could you find someone to clear this mess up before someone breaks their neck."

My God it's her...how did that happen? I'm so embarrassed, but then she can catch me when I fall anytime. She's even more beautiful close up, but she's different from last night somehow, she just bellowed at that poor assistant.

The compassion is back in her eyes as she takes a seat next to me, looking straight into my eyes she's saying something about incompetence, but I can't quiet concentrate, she is so distracting.

"Would you like me to get you something to drink? You seem lost somehow?"

"Oh, really I'm fine, just a little embarrassed," I manage to squeak out. This gets worse, I must sound pathetic.

"Well, as long as you're alright. Did you have a question for me? I remember your face from last night."

Yes, like how would you like to come out with me and spend like forever with me? Stop it, I think to myself. I'm still engaged to Grace, which reminds me I must sort things out there.

"Well, I just thought, you know, after last night this sounds ridiculous."

"Not at all, Mr Edwards...go on, I'm all ears."

How did she know my name was Mr Edwards? She is touching my arm with her hand; it feels really hot, her hand that is...it's sending a tingling sensation through me. It's weird but kind of comforting somehow.

"How did you know my name was Russell Edwards? Did you look me up or something?"

"I don't look anyone up, Mr Edwards. My information comes from the most reliable source."

"Who might that be?"

"Mr Edwards, I'm a medium. I work with guides that come from higher sources than earth, and when I'm on stage, I'm joined by many spirits and guides. You look lost

11

again…look, I don't usually, but well, here's a card. It has my address and telephone number on it. Rose does a group at my house where you can learn all about the spirit world and the things I do."

"Do you join the group?" *What am I saying?* I don't do support groups or the spirit world.

"I try to join as often as possible. I built the healing/meditation room in my garden, to give me a place to meditate. And then Rose suggested doing groups and workshops, so I let her use the space to help people connect. I'm not here to persuade you either way, a lot of the time people are afraid of the unknown and what I do. Which is so sad in my opinion, as these higher being are there to help and don't wish anyone any harm. However, I feel that you would benefit from the healing sessions Rose runs, sometimes just sitting in the atmosphere, watching and listening can bring a person inner peace."

"I suppose Rosanna would like to join some kind of group."

"Well, now is not really the time to discuss this further. Call me and I can give you dates and events when Rosanna and you can join in."

"That would be really nice, thank you."

"Excuse me just one moment, I just need to sort out where this painting is going, I like to make sure my paintings are displayed in the right place."

"Can I join you?"

"Of course, this way."

I follow her into one of the exhibition rooms enjoying the view of her arse. She starts talking to one of the assistants and is explaining to them how she would like the painting displayed. I, for another matter, am fascinated with the lady; she looks at them differently, somehow to the way in which she looks at me. She seems to be happy with her display, and then she turns to me and says: "Would you like to catch a coffee in the cafeteria, then I can tell you a little bit about the history of The Tate Gallery?"

"Yes, that would be nice. Is this one of your paintings?"

I would like to spend as much time with this lady as possible.

"It is, I painted that one whilst on holiday in Paris many years ago."

Her expression changes again, her eyes almost go cold like she's remembering an unhappy time.

"It certainly is a beautiful piece of art."

"The place was fantastic; the company I was with not so much. Shall we get that coffee?"

"Yes, sure."

As we walk to the cafeteria she points out various sculptures, paintings, and mentions various famous artists. I'm intrigued by what she tells me, although I have to admit I know very little about art.

"How do you take your coffee, Mr Edwards?"

"White no sugar. Here, let me get these, and please, call me Russell."

With that she looks at me with hardness.

"Mr Edwards. Um, Russell, I'm an independent lady and I'm more than capable of buying two coffees."

"OK, I'm usually used to paying for things when I go for a drink with a lady."

"Not with this lady you don't. Find a table. That one over there will do, it has a nice view."

Well, she told me. I feel like I've been put in my place somehow. That doesn't change my opinion of this lady though, she is so changeable but so Goddam gorgeous with it.

"This sure is a magnificent building."

"Yes it is special. It was originally a prison."

"Really, it doesn't look much like a prison now."

"This building was designed by Sidney R.J. Smith and has had many major extensions over the years to house the various different British artists work. It also has a painting conservation where specialists preserve precious artwork."

"That's interesting. So how did it get the name Tate Gallery?"

"Henry Tate was an industrialist who made his fortune as a sugar refiner. He offered his collection of British art to the nation, but unfortunately there was no space in the National Gallery. So hence the opening of Tate Gallery around 1932. Lots of British artists work in-house today, and the Gallery holds various collections, international, modern and contemporary."

"So, what got you into art?"

"I've always loved to paint; I find it relaxing. Do you like art, Russell?"

"Never been able to paint or draw myself, but I do appreciate the beauty in sculptures and paintings." *I very much appreciate the beauty of the person sitting opposite me*, I think to myself.

"So, what brought you to the Gallery today?"

"Well, I'm embarrassed to say really, but I'm not one to lie. After last night, I looked you up and was curious I guess." And sort of hoping to see you again.

"I see, well that doesn't usually happen."

"You mean crazy men don't follow you around?" God she is so beautiful when she laughs.

"No, I don't think I've ever had a crazy man look me up before."

"I find that hard to believe." More fool them.

Her mobile starts to ring interrupting our conversation.

"Excuse me. I need to get this. Hello, Leigh-Anna. Yes, is it that time already? OK, I'll be out shortly. Well, Russell, I'm afraid I must be going."

I feel a stab of disappointment that our meeting is coming to an end and hope she doesn't see the disappointment in my face.

"I'll walk out with you."

"OK."

We make our way down the steps of the Gallery onto the street and towards a rather butch looking lady, when,

"Oh, no you don't!" she shouts out to the rather skinny young man who's just tried to pinch her handbag. Before I know it, she's pulled his arm behind his back and pushed him to the floor. I reach for my mobile phone as her driver and myself kneel at her side on the floor.

"Mr Edwards, there is no need to involve the police, I have this under control!" she bellows at me. A security guard from the gallery also joins us. "Leigh-Anna, be a darling and take this young man into the cafeteria and find out why he feels the need to take someone else's belongings. If his reasons are genuine, then feed the skinny thing, he looks like he could do with a good meal. I'll wait for you by the water over there."

"OK, Penny, as you wish."

She turns to talk to the security guard, then makes her way towards the Thames.

I follow her over to a bench and we sit looking out over the Thames. Lost for words to start with, I finally manage to ask, "How did you manage to take that guy down?" I am amazed not only by her beauty but also by her strength.

"Oh, I had self-defence lessons. I know how to look after myself."

"Well, you certainly sorted him out. But why did you not want me to call the police?"

"Russell, in what way would that help that young man?"

"I'm lost; I don't think I quite follow you. Surely, he should be done for what he tried to do?"

"I understand what you are saying, and many would agree with you, but don't you see that young man needs help not discipline."

The sadness and compassion is in her eyes as she talks to me about the young man, who just tried to rob her. I would like to have thumped him one.

"I think I'd find it hard to be so forgiving."

"Don't you think it is kind of sad really how someone is so desperate that just to find their next meal they have to steal from someone? He was so young, and so very thin, something must have gone really wrong in his life for him to resort to such things."

"Well, I guess I can kind of see what you are saying."

We sit next to each other for some time lost in our own thoughts and just staring out at the water, when finally, her driver returns.

"Are you ready to go now?"

"Yes, we'll pick Barney up on the way. Well, it's been an interesting afternoon, Mr Edwards. Maybe we'll meet again sometime."

"Thank you, and I very much hope to see you again." I walk over to the car with her and she shakes my hand, and then I watch and wave as she drives away. I don't know about settling my curiosity, I think it has grown somewhat by this mysterious beauty. How I long to know her better, and who's Barney? I secretly hope she doesn't already have a partner.

 ===== *X* =====

Chapter Four

"Well, Dad, this sure is a great house right on the broads. Lovely view over the water from the master suite. When do you think you'll get a boat sorted?"

"I was hoping to rebuild the one the Talbot's left behind, but looking at it, it's beyond repair. I think we'll get the house redecorated first, then I can get someone to take a look at the boat. Mrs West, the lady next door, has invited us to dinner tonight, maybe she will know someone?"

Now that name's familiar, surely she couldn't be related to the famous Mystic Pen. God, I can't get the woman out of my head, so beautiful and strong. I must try to distract myself with something other than Penelope West. I haven't seen the woman for a week now, but she still occupies my thoughts. Fishing? Yes, that's it, I should keep my mind from thinking about her.

"What time are we supposed to be going to dinner, only I thought I might get some fishing in before getting changed?"

"About five, check with your mother. Why has Grace not come with you this weekend?"

With a loud sigh I answer my father, hoping he won't be too disappointed, "She made some sort of feeble excuse about working."

"Things not going too good then. Anything I can help with, son?"

"I don't know, Dad. I don't want to disappoint anyone but my feelings have changed. She won't set a date for the wedding and makes every excuse under the sun not to spend time with me. To be really honest, if I didn't know better, I'd say she has found someone else." *Maybe I have.*

"If it's not right, son, then you must sort it out. Everyone will understand. Marriage is a lifetime thing, so you must be sure. I like Grace, but if truth been known, I've never seen the spark between the two of you. We just want you to be happy and if you're not, then change it, son."

"Thanks, Dad."

"Penny, how lovely to see you, and you're looking so well. How's this big fellow of yours? Sky will be pleased to see him."

"Aunt Megan, how are you. Let me see you."

I take my aunt in my arms and give her the biggest squeeze ever, then stand back and take a look at her.

"Yes, you're sure looking great. I see the air here really suits you."

"Oh, Penny, you're such a darling. Buying this house for me and doing it all up, you know I didn't bring you up for you to reward me so. It's such a lovely gift, I still have to pinch myself every morning when I wake up you know."

Aunt Meg, such a remarkable lady to which I owe everything, she shows her appreciation with such tears in her eyes.

"Anything for you, your happiness and wishes are always my top priority. Think nothing of it; besides, I can get some lovely pictures painted here, with all this natural beauty."

"Come on in, Sky is dying to see you both. Oh, I have new neighbours next door; I hope you don't mind but I've invited them to dinner tonight. Sort of a welcome to the neighbourhood gesture. They seem really lovely people. I'm sure you'll like them."

"Mrs Talbot finally sold up then."

"Yes, dear. I think she found it too hard to live there after Mr Talbot died, bless her."

"Shame isn't it; they were such a dear lovely couple. I guess after fifty years of marriage, any one of us would find it hard. I feel for her. Did she leave her address so that you can stay in touch?"

"Yes, I've already received a letter, telling me all about her new home. She's going to invite us both round once she's got the place sorted."

"That'll be nice. I'll just get my things unpacked, then I'll be right down for a coffee."

"You didn't need to bring the kitchen sink with you. After all, the bedroom that you done for yourself is full of your stuff already!" she shouts up the stairs after me.

"You know me, Aunt Meg, a girl can never have too many clothes. You never know who you might meet or see!" I shout laughing back at her.

Well the day sure had passed quickly, after catching up with Aunt Megan and then checking the boat over to make sure everything was ready for tomorrow. However, I needn't have bothered, as Jack who helps with the maintenance of the house and boat had already cleaned and sorted the boat knowing I was coming. Him and his wife are delightful people, always checking on Aunt Megan for me and keeping me informed of everything... not that I'd let her know they're my spies. I laugh to myself as I slip into my dress and finish applying my makeup, when suddenly, the doorbell rings.

I heard my aunt answer the door. "Mr and Mrs Edwards, how lovely to see you, and this must be your son Russell and daughter Rosanna. I've heard so much about you both already, all good though."

"Please, Megan, call us Sylvia and Michael. It was most kind of you to ask us over for dinner."

"Think nothing of it, Florrie my good friend helped with all the cooking. Her husband Jack, helps with the maintenance outside here and Florrie loves to keep busy with me. Of course, we keep each other busy gossiping as my niece tells me... who will be joining us shortly."

I walk down the stairs and almost stop halfway, my eyes meeting his once again. It can't be, but it is. *Soul, what are you up to?* I think to myself.

"Russell, we meet again."

"Penelope, how lovely to see you."

Rosanna pushes in front of me, "Hello, it's great to see

you again."

I can't believe it, she looks absolutely stunning in her red dress, which clings to every curve and by God has she got curves. Bright red lipstick, and those lips I could only imagine kissing…and heeled shoes. God, at this rate how am I going to get through dinner? My heart is racing and I'm uncomfortable in the trouser department again. I can't take my eyes of her as she's talking to Rosanna, then speaks to my mother and father, I couldn't tell you a word they were saying. That smile of hers it just lights up the room. No woman has ever made me feel this way before. I'm completely transfixed.

"Come through, Russell."

Gladly, I'd follow that arse anywhere. *Stop it, Russell,* I tell myself, *behave.*

"OK, this sure is a nice house. Has your aunt lived here long?"

My God my voice sounds so hoarse. What is wrong with me?

"About eighteen months now."

"Well, it sure looks like a great place to live."

We take our seats at the table and begin to eat; however, my appetite is on other things, as I can't take my eyes of the beautiful lady sitting opposite me. Megan seems to be telling my mother about the local area and giving her information on places to visit, whilst my Dad seems to be talking away to Penelope about boats and the water. I can tell by the look on her face that she knows the broads well and is enjoying their conversation, she's telling him about someone who could help with the boat. I on the other hand can't concentrate on anything other than her and every now and then she glances up and catches my eye, and each time I feel her foot catch my leg under the table, sending shivers and electricity down my spine.

Somehow, I manage to get through the dinner in one piece, although the feeling in my groin is not easing at all. *What is it about this woman?* Her aunt starts to talk about someone called William and with that Penelope's eyes turn to stone. She excuses herself from the table saying something about letting Barney and Sky out into the garden. Yes, I remember, now who's this Barney guy? And who's William? He sure seems to have got Penelope rattled, and by the look she gives her aunt, she's not best pleased that she's brought the subject up.

"Mind if I join you?" I find myself asking.

"Of course not, this way."

She takes me through to the kitchen area where two big German Shepherd dogs come bounding towards us wagging their tails. With a command they both sit and she bends down and makes a real fuss of them, but when the tan and black one sees me, he eyes me and starts to growl.

"Barney, friend," she commands.

He is obviously very obedient. He walks over to me and circles around me as if he's checking me out, sniffing all the time. "Is it OK to fuss him?" I ask.

"Once he knows you, he will be fine. Barney can be a bit protective of me, so let him sniff your hand and then he will be fine."

So this is Barney. "He sure is a magnificent dog, and who's this one?" I ask while fussing the white German Sheppard, who has decided she doesn't want to be left out.

"That's Sky, Aunt Megan's dog. She is more placid although protective of Megan. It's in their nature to protect their master."

Sky was now rolling around the floor allowing me to rub her belly while Barney was sitting between me and Penelope, staring at me out of the corner of his eye, and leaning against my leg. "Barney, I know what you're doing." One word from her and he stops leaning against me.

"Come on then," Penelope says. Sky starts bounding around the kitchen all excitedly, and she can't get to the door quick enough. Barney follows, although he still seems wary of my presence. "He will be just as soppy with you once he gets to know you."

I'm not so sure of that, although he won't frighten me away. She kicks off her heels and leaves them at the back door, changing into some flats, she is still at least five-foot five inches tall and all legs. We make our way out into the garden area were the dogs excitedly run round playing together, and we make our way through an arch at the bottom of the garden, which leads to the broads. After looking around and seeing no one is about fishing, Penelope picks up a stick and throws it into the water. Barney's first in followed by Sky as they compete to get the stick.

Once again I find myself transfixed watching this lady smiling and encouraging both dogs. I decide to join in the game, and both of us are throwing sticks into the water and encouraging them back to us, laughing together. Then Penelope calls the dogs out of the water once their interest subsides and both dogs shake themselves out soaking both of us, which just makes us laugh all the more. We settle down on a bench next to each other looking out over the water, both of us looking rather damp, while the dogs settle at our feet panting. Could this be any more relaxing?

I keep looking over at her and the way that dress is now clinging to her body showing her underwear and spectacular curves. My trousers are more than tight with the constant throbbing of my cock. I want to lean over and kiss those beautiful red lips. Then she puts a hand on my thigh and says, "It's such a beautiful evening, I love spending time here."

"I'm looking forward to spending more time here too," I manage to say rather huskily.

She leans over towards me and I close my eyes; for a minute I think she's going to kiss me, when she stands and says, "We'd better get these dogs dried and back to the others before they send a search party out looking for us."

I stand and follow her through the arch and up the garden, two exhausted pooches in tow. Once back at the house, we dry the dogs as best we can and when Megan and my mother come into the kitchen, they look at us both and laugh. "What happened to you two? Did you go swimming with the dogs?"

We look at each other and burst out laughing. She is so beautiful when she laughs. "We were just going to fill the dishwasher up," Megan said. "I did tell Sylvia that Florrie would sort it all out tomorrow, but she insisted on doing something."

"That's my mother for you, not one to sit around for long. I tell you what, why don't you go for a walk in the garden and I'll sort the dishes while Penelope gets changed."

"I'm fine, Russell, please call me Penny. Why don't we do this together; it will be quicker."

"If you're sure."

We start to rinse some of the plates and fill the dish washer, our hands touching as they meet sending a tingling sensation through my body. Occasionally, our eyes meet, and the look of passion that must have been in my eyes I hope is not too obvious. Once our task is done we make our way back to join the others.

"Well, it's been a lovely evening, I do hope you will join us next time once we've got the place sorted out. I can't wait for tomorrow," Sylvia says.

"Oh, Penny, I hope you don't mind but I've asked them to join us on the boat tomorrow. I know you want to get some painting in, we won't disturb you we promise."

"Do you fish, Russell?"

"Yes."

"Good, bring your rods. I'll paint you fishing up the broads with the windmill in the background. We will leave at dawn."

"Sounds good, until tomorrow then. I look forward to it."

I don't know what you're playing at, Soul, but I can't get involved with someone, you know that. 'This will be different, trust me.' *I trust you with my life, but you know how I feel about men.* 'You need to live your life, just trust us on this one. It will be different this time.' *I don't know*, I say to my strong guide as I get ready for bed that night, although I do know that my strong guide will never let me down.

===== *X* =====

Chapter Five

We knock on the door of Mrs West's beautiful house at the crack of dawn. I can't wait to see Penny again. The woman makes my heart beat faster and faster. I sure had a job sleeping, I kept thinking about the delightful company I was with yesterday evening. At least I get to spend the whole day with her today; this weekend break just gets better and better. I can't remember the last time I laughed so much. Maybe I'll even find out some more about the beautiful lady who I lost sleep over last night.

"Sylvia, Russell. How delightful to see you both again? Where is Michael and Rosanna?"

"Unfortunately, Michael had to take Rosanna back to St Albans. Her friend's grandmother died during the night and Rosanna wanted to be there for her friend. She was going to drive back on her own but Michael wouldn't hear of it."

"Ah that's sad, I do hope her friend is OK. Just the four of us then, and two hairy mutts. Come through to the kitchen, Penny is just loading the rest of the picnic into the baskets and then we're off."

"Good morning, Sylvia and Russell, how are you today? I do hope Rosanna's friend is OK?"

"Good morning, Penny dear, you look delightful. Doesn't she look lovely, Russell?"

"Yes, perfect, how are you this morning?"

"Never been better. I've loaded my easels and brushes already, just need to take the food down and then we're ready for the off. Here, Russell, take this. I'll take these two, let's go."

We all follow Penny down the garden and to the side where a spectacular looking boat awaits us. I didn't notice it last night but then maybe it was stored in the building at the side of the house, and I wonder if Penny got it out herself or if she has someone look after it for her. That leaves the question who is going to drive the boat? I know she has a driver who drives her to and from events, but driving a boat must be different.

I can't keep my eyes of her and I'm wondering how she knew about Rosanna's friend. That's it, she must have heard us telling her aunt about it when we arrived. She puts the picnic baskets down and with one jump she's on board. She helps my mother and her aunt on board and then looks over at me.

"Russell, be a love and pass me those baskets." I do as I'm asked then she holds out her hand for me. Automatically, I take her hand, glad of her touch, it sends a tingling sensation up my arm. As I step on board, somehow I manage to slip and I end up virtually on top of her.

"Mr Edwards, you seem to make a habit of slipping into my arms," she's laughs as she pushes herself up. I on the other hand, would rather stay where I am, wrapped in her arms, my pulse is thumping, my heart is about to bounce out of my chest and my cock has gone uncomfortably large against my trousers. I hope no one notices the effect this woman has on me.

"Well, Miss West, there's no place I'd rather be."

But, shouldn't it be the man that helps the ladies on board a boat and carries these heavy picnic baskets, I think to myself. It doesn't seem right to me somehow.

Once Penny has shown us around 'Peggy' (her boat, which I find out is named after her late mother), my mother and Megan start to unload the picnic baskets into the fridge, while Barney and Sky take their positions up front sitting looking out over the water. Penny gets into the captain's seat and starts the engine. "Everyone ready," she calls, and with that we're off.

After checking the waterway is clear, we head west up river. Penny steers the boat to the right hand side of the river with great ease. She even looks good in casual wear.

"Where are we heading?"

"Well, I was going to head east towards a small place called Acle and paint the windmill, but I'll save that for next time. I thought we'd head towards the River Bure and go to Coltishaw. Should only take us just over an hour and half to get there. There is a private mooring there where we can stop and you can catch fish. There is perch, rud, roach, pike, and carp in the water. It will also be the perfect spot to paint you fishing, the water and bushes in the background."

Another boat passes on the other side of the river and Penny smiles and waves to the driver.

"Do you know them?" I ask.

"No, just being polite. You find that here, most of the other river users wave politely."

"So what else is at Coltishaw?"

"Just up the road from the private mooring is a pub and shop. I thought your mother and my aunt might like to take a walk up to the shop and have a look around while I'm painting and you're fishing."

"My mother would love that."

"We can have our picnic on the picnic benches by the private mooring, and then maybe go to the pub later for some dinner before heading back. We may as well make the most of the sunshine."

"Sounds good to me."

We make our way slowly towards Wroxham Bridge and I feel slightly tense. I wonder how Penny is going to get this large boat underneath this small bridge, but she does so with great ease and expertise.

"Have you always driven big boats on these broads, Penny?"

"I used to come here every year with my aunt and uncle for holidays as a child. My uncle used to show me how to maintain and drive safely on the waterway. Have you never been here before?"

"Only once before; most of our holidays were abroad when I was growing up. When we were independent and could look after ourselves, Mum and Dad came on a boating holiday here on their own. They liked it so much they decided to retire here."

We cruise slowly up river waving at the occasional boat that passes by and turn on to a more secluded waterway with nothing but trees surrounding us.

"If we're lucky we may see a kingfisher. Keep your eyes out; they are beautiful birds."

It really is a beautiful place. I feel very relaxed.

"Would you like a go at steering? This is a quiet part of the river."

"Well if you're sure."

"Of course, there's nothing to it. Besides, if your Dad gets a boat, you'll need to know how to drive them about when you come for holidays."

I take the wheel feeling slightly nervous.

"What do I do?"

Penny leans over me, her breast brushes my arm. That's it. I'm rock hard again, pulse racing at this rate…how am I going to be able to concentrate on what she's saying. She stands up straight.

"Got all that?"

"What, um, perhaps you'd better talk me through it again."

She points out all the dials in front of me again, her breast brushing my arm as she reaches over, but this time I just about manage to concentrate on what she's telling me. She tells me about the speed restrictions and rules of the waterway. After showing me all the dials she takes a seat next to me, her leg slightly touching mine. God, I think I'm on fire or I've been electrocuted or something. The sensation is out of this world. This woman does something to me that's for sure.

"If you're OK for a minute, I'll just go and fetch us a coffee."

"Coffee, yes that would be nice." Should keep my mind

from wandering.

She'd only been gone for a few seconds and there was a boat approaching on the other side of the river. My heart starts to pound and I'm feeling slightly nervous. *Keep right*, I say to myself.

"Penny, there's a boat coming towards us."

She comes over to me sensing my panic. Leaning over me from behind, she holds the steering wheel with me. Her breasts are pushed into my back and both her arms are either side of me. That's it, I've had it, how's a man to concentrate. My cock is so uncomfortable, my pulse is racing, my heart is about to jump out of my chest. She smells so delightful and her touch is electrifying.

"There, that wasn't so bad, you'll get used to it," she said. "Am I alright to get that coffee now? Russell, are you OK?"

"Um, yes I think so," I say huskily, feeling that I might be even better if I could take her through to that bedroom and fuck her brains out. Better make out that it was just the thought of banging into the boat that was coming the other way. *What is wrong with me?*

"I was just a little worried I'd run into that boat. Wouldn't want to damage your boat."

"As long as you stay steadily to the right you'll be fine; I'll get those coffees now."

"OK," I manage to squeak out.

We had been travelling up river for well over an hour now. Megan and my mother seem to be getting along like they've known each other for years. It's nice to see my mother relaxed and enjoying herself. Penny has stayed close by my side, allowing me to steer the boat and giving me the odd bit of help every now and then. I don't think I've ever felt this close to someone in my whole life. We start to approach some houses on the right hand side and Penny gets up.

"We are here. If you steer the boat slowly to the side, I'll jump off and pull her in. Just turn the engine off once

29

I've tied her up, OK."

As I approach the riverbank, Penny jumps on land and pulls the boat in, and with expertise she ties the boat securely to a bolder and I cut the engine.

"There, all safe and sound. Well done, Mr Edwards, it looks like we'll have turned you into a captain before your father gets that boat of his." I can't help but laugh.

Penny sets about unloading her easel, paint and brushes and I set up my fishing rod and rest at the side of the boat. Penny pulls two loungers off the boat and sets them up for my mother and her aunt. I did offer to help but it seems to me that Penny likes to take charge of things, so I reluctantly allow her to get them both comfortable. I take my seat at the water's edge and watch my float lazily while my mother seems to be chatting away quietly to Penny's aunt. Barney has taken it upon himself to lay down right by my side and Sky is happily lazing with him. I don't think I've ever been so relaxed; *I could get used to this*, I think to myself.

After catching about five little fish in a row, Megan announces that she's taking my mother for a walk along the riverbank, up to the shop to have a look around. I look round and see that Penny is painting away. I reel my float in and wonder if she'd like a glass of wine. I take it upon myself to go on the boat and pour out two glasses of wine. When I take one over to Penny, she covers her painting over and takes the glass of wine I hand her. "Thanks. An artist never reveals her work till it's complete." She smiles at me. "Want something to eat?" she asks, and then heads over to the boat and comes back with a picnic rug and basket.

She lays the rug down and then asks me to join her. I notice that Sky and Barney are now sitting alongside the picnic rug with wanting eyes on the picnic basket. Penny throws them both a chew. "That should keep them happy for a while. So, Russell, tell me about Grace?"

"What do you want to know?"

"Well, you haven't sorted things out yet and you didn't seem happy to be with her the night of my show."

"Well, I met Grace a few years ago at one of my mother's dinner parties. Couldn't say it was love at first sight, but she seemed a nice enough person at the time. We went out on a few dates, my mother seemed to like her, and I thought I was falling in love with her so I asked her to marry me."

"There is a 'but' in there somewhere." Penny makes eye contact with me and I think to myself, *but I met you and my feelings have changed.*

After a long pause, I tell Penny how my feelings for Grace have changed and that I think she is seeing someone else, but I don't want to let everyone down. I'm careful to omit the part about the fact I'm starting to fall in love with the lady lazing by my side, who I feel like I've known all of my life and whose company I enjoy more than anyone I've ever met.

"Well, it seems to me that you would be letting yourself down if you married someone you didn't love?"

"I never looked at it that way before, but I guess you're right."

She leans over close to me, and feeds me a strawberry while looking into each other's eyes. Just then, my mother and her aunt return, both looking at us curiously.

"If I didn't know better I'd say you two were lovers," my mother says with a frown.

Penny simply replies: "I was just telling Russell how lovely these strawberries taste."

"We got hungry so started the picnic without you," I say.

Penny gets up and goes over to the boat and comes back with another picnic basket and lays a load of food out for my mother and her aunt, who have taken to their loungers again. I can feel my mother's eyes on me with silent questioning in them. I guess I'm going to have to tell her how I'm feeling.

After the picnic, Penny returns to her painting and I return fishing, wondering how I'm going to tell my mother that I intend to break my engagement with Grace once I return to St Albans. Although she is quietly reading her book, I can see her out of the corner of my eye occasionally glancing my way with questioning eyes, and I'm wondering if she is surprised or disappointed in me.

After reloading the boat, we make our way a little further up river to the pub Penny was talking about last night. We spend the evening in the pub talking and laughing over a delightful meal. "Your aunt tells me you're a medium, Penny. How long have you done mediumship?" my mother asks.

"It's been with me all of my life."

"I thought vicars were against that sort of thing?"

"Most are, they feel that once a person's physical body has died, you should allow the soul to rest and not disturb them. I never disturb a soul, they choose to come to me and use me to give messages and reassurance to loved ones they have left behind. Sometimes they have left earth in difficult circumstances or suddenly, and haven't had a proper chance to say goodbye."

"Interesting, can you call someone to you?" my mother asks.

"A soul will only come to me if they wish to pass on a message; you can't force them to come."

My mother seems to be lost in her own thoughts as we make our way back to the boat. Penny puts a hand on my mother's shoulder and says: "Our loved ones are only a thought away." She looks into my mother's eyes and says something I can't quiet hear, and my mother nods at her.

The ride back seems to take longer, and somehow we seem to be on the river surrounded by bushes for a long time before we finally reach Megan's home. Once Penny has secured the boat we unload the boat and make our way to

Megan's house. Megan asks politely if we would like to join them for a coffee, but my mother looks really tired and declines the offer, saying that next time Megan must come to us and what a delightful day she has had. As she heads to the door she turns to Penny and says: "I think I'll come for that healing session soon."

Penny nods and says that before she heads home the next day, she will pop round and do some healing on my mother.

"That would be great, thanks, and thanks for the wonderful day."

I am left wondering why my mother needs healing and what Penny had said to my mother earlier.

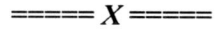

===== X =====

Chapter Six

I have been back from my weekend break now for a few weeks and have been so busy at work that I haven't seen anything of Penny, and Grace is not answering any of my calls. So, that's it, I've had enough. I'm making my way round there in five minutes, just as soon as I've shut my computer down. I'm fed up with having to deal with a half-hearted engagement. I have other more pressing pursuits to follow up. I must see Penny again, but the question is will she want to see me. I can't stop thinking of the weekend away a few weeks ago, and what a wonderful time I had in her company. That's it, I'll break off this shambles of an engagement and then make my way round to Penny's and tell her how I feel…at least I hope I have the guts to tell her how I feel.

I make my way up the drive of the house I'm having redecorated ready for when I'm supposed to be married, and wonder what I'm going to do with this house. I guess I'll have to sell it and buy something else. I don't like the place much anyway; it had been more Grace's choice and not my taste really, and she should be here overseeing the renovations.

As I approach, I notice a rather tatty looking car parked next to Grace's on the drive and wonder who it belongs to. It certainly isn't anyone I know. It could be a workman's car, but shouldn't they all have gone home by now, after all, it is Friday evening? Maybe they are going over some plans or something, but shouldn't Grace have told me if there was something to discuss. See, that's exactly why this just won't work. She never tells me anything, but she is quick enough to spend my money.

I open the door quietly and as I step inside, I see a trail of clothing littered all the way up the stairs and my heart sinks. I can hear voices and giggling coming from upstairs. Do I really want to follow that trail of clothes? I already know what's going on. Slowly, I walk upstairs and swing open the door to the master bedroom. There is my so-called fiancé stripped naked in bed with some rough looking man. She turns to look at me stumbles out of the bed grabbing a sheet with her. "Russell, I can explain," she says as I turn and make my way back down the stairs.

"Don't bother, Grace, it's over. Leave your key at the door on your way out."

I get back in my car and start to drive, I don't know where I'm going, just anywhere away from here.

It feels like I've been driving aimlessly around for a long time now, just feeling numb. I'm not sure how I'm supposed to feel, as I was going to break up with her anyway. I pull over into a garage and get a bottle of water, but when I pull out my wallet to pay, a card falls out of it. I look at Penny's card blankly and wonder if she would do something like that to me. *No*, a quiet voice says in my mind. My mobile rings. Great, it's Grace.

"What do you want, Grace?"

"I was going to tell you, but never found the right time."

"So you just sleep with anyone in our supposed honeymoon bed!" I bellow down the phone as I walk back to the car. "If you didn't want to be with me, then why get engaged? You've been avoiding me for weeks. Funny how you can sleep with some rough arsehole, yet you wanted to save all that for when we were married."

"I know, Russ, please, I'm really sorry…just come back to the house and we'll discuss it."

"Don't you dare call me, Russ! Get out of my house and out of my life." With that I hang up.

I've been back in the car for a while now and I'm aimlessly driving towards a big gate. I press the intercom button and the gate swings open, and as I drive up this long driveway, I'm wondering how I managed to get here. I approach some kind of water fountain in front of the big house and I can see Penny waiting at the door for me with Barney, who appears to be all alert. I park the car and climb out feeling really deflated.

"Russell, come on in, my love. You found out the hard way then."

I look at Penny blankly, not sure what to say. She takes me in her arms and cuddles me really tightly rubbing my back, and I bury my head in her hair taking in her beautiful scent. *I could stay this way forever*, I think to myself feeling completely at peace in her arms. She pulls back and looks into my eyes with compassion. Taking hold of my hand she leads me into what looks like a magnificent lounge, while Barney follows closely behind, sniffing and checking me out.

She leads me over to the long sofa and I plonk down. Barney immediately jumps on it and lays his head in my lap, looking at me out of the corner of his eye as if to say "cheer up mate".

"Have you eaten?" Penny asks.

I stare at her and shake my head, not quite sure how I'm feeling at this precise moment. She leaves the room and I'm thinking, *how did I get here?* And what am I doing?

Penny returns with some food and lays it down on the coffee table. Barney jumps down and she gives him a chew to keep him occupied. "You must eat, Russell."

I nod and take a few bites of the meal laid out in front of me.

"Want to talk about it? I do know how it feels you know, it happened to me loads of times when…" She doesn't finish her sentence, but her face does turn hard at what seems to be an unpleasant memory, at which point I find myself telling her the whole story.

"So you see, I'm not sure how I feel about it all really. I was going to break up with her anyway. I knew she was seeing someone else, but knowing and actually seeing her with someone is kind of different I guess."

We stare at each other and then I continue: "I know she

wasn't the one for me anyway, so I kind of feel relieved she gave me a way out. Does that sound wrong?"

"Guilt talking huh, no it doesn't sound wrong at all. I know exactly how you feel. How many partners have you had, Russell?"

Where did that come from? "Three in total, although I haven't been with anyone for a while now." *What kind of question was that?*

She leans over to me and I think she's going to kiss me; her hand is on my knee and her face is right close to mine, our eyes lock and she says, "Same as me. Look, I know there's some sort of spark between us, so shall we just have some fun and forget about all our worries for now."

"Every time you touch me I'm on fire. I've never felt like this before. The other weekend was just one of the best weekends I've ever had."

She stands up and pulls me up with her.

She leads me out of the lounge and up some stairs. Pushing open a door, she pulls me around in front of her and kisses me passionately while undressing the buttons on my shirt. God, I think I've died and gone to heaven. I open my eyes as she pulls back slightly and I try to take in my surroundings, and then she starts to push me backwards towards a big four-poster bed. Before I know it, my shirt is thrown across the room and my trousers are down at my ankles, along with my boxers. She's looking at me now with passion in her eyes and she pushes me gently backwards and I fall on to the bed.

I struggle out of my trousers as she pulls her dress up over her head revealing her sexy underwear. *God, this woman is sex on legs*, my cock is rock hard and I think I must be dreaming. What did I do to deserve such a beautiful lady? She removes her underwear and pushing me back so that I'm lying flat on the bed and I'm wondering with anticipation what she's going to do to me. Before I know it she's on top of me, kissing me wildly and I find myself willingly kissing her back with a newfound desire that I never knew existed.

She takes me inside her slowly to start with, then more fiercely, pushing on to me, laying downwards to start with. I can feel myself swell as if I'm about to come when she pulls out of me and I'm left thinking, *My God, no.*

"You can't come before I'm ready, Mr Edwards. It's so much better to come together, don't you think?"

She sits up on me and is teasing my cock with her sexual parts, rubbing up against me. I throw my head back and groan with anticipation, capturing her breasts in both my hands. I caress them whilst she teases my cock and rubs her hands through my chest, almost scratching me with her nails. I don't care at this point. I'm at her mercy. She can do what she likes with me. The sensations I'm feeling right now are out of this world.

She takes me back within her deeply and is riding me hard, really hard and when I think I'm going to explode, she withdraws again, teasing me and saying: "I'm not ready yet."

Will this torture ever end? I think to myself.

I try to sit up and push back into her, but she simply pushes me back down.

"I'm in control of this, and I will tell you when you can come. That won't be until I'm ready, OK."

I'm completely breathless and dumbfounded. I can't get enough. "More!" I squeal out.

"Are you sure you can take it?"

"Anything," I beg, caressing her breasts wildly while she continues to tease my cock.

She takes me within her again just brushing over the head of my cock and pushes gently down on me. I try to raise my hips to push in deeper and harder, but she manages to hold me still somehow.

"My pace, Mr Edwards, not yours," she says then rides me slowly and seductively to start with, and then increases her pace and begins to ride me harder and harder until…

"I'm going to come!" I bellow. She pulls off me again and I scream, "What are doing to me, woman."

"I'm simply teaching you control, Mr Edwards, and

when I'm ready we will come together. You wouldn't want to disappoint me now would you?" She's teasing my cock again and slightly digs her nails into my chest.

I'm panting and practically begging her for release. I've never experienced such frustration and pleasure at the same time before. She lays on me again and kisses me hard while running her fingers through my hair slightly, tugging as she's pushing back on to my cock, this time allowing me to move with her and together we find a steady rhythm. I wrap my arms around her and try to slow her slightly, but she's having none of it. Speeding up she takes me fully within her, and that's it, I explode screaming out her name at the same time as she finds her own release.

"How was that?" she whispers in my ear.

"Wow, heavenly," I manage to squeak.

She gently pulls off me and lays by my side, stroking my chest and I leave my arm wrapped around her. "How did you manage to control me like that?" I manage to say, once I'd caught my breath.

"You really want to know?"

"I want to know everything about you."

"I'm sure you wouldn't want to know everything; you'd run a mile if you did. So many times in the past I had to endure unsatisfied sex. One man in particular wanting to have sex all his own way, always coming just before I was about to, and leaving me wanting more and being frustrated. So, my last partner I used to experiment with."

"In what way?"

"By making him wait until I was ready to come."

"You can make me wait anytime you like."

"Did you enjoy yourself, Russell? I know I did."

"Um, I'd like to do that again," I say, caressing her arm with my fingers.

"Well, I like my men to be fully hard, not halfway there...so I'll give you till tomorrow to recover."

"Right, tomorrow it is then."

"If I say so," she says, smiling down at me.

I can't help but laugh; this woman is something else. The kind of woman I could easily spend the rest of my life with; however, I wonder what she meant when she said I'd run a mile. Never, nothing she could tell me would make me run from her, I think to myself as I fall blissfully asleep next to the lady who has me completely at her mercy.

Chapter Seven

I wake to the sound of Russell snoring softly next to me and glance over at the hunk lying next to me. *What have I done?* He'd never be interested in staying with someone like me if he knew the truth. Yet there is something there between us. I can feel it; it's like nothing I've ever felt before. He is so handsome, so why would he want to be with me anyway. *Now, Penny,* I scold myself, *why wouldn't he want to be with you?* I can think of loads of reasons. I must let Barney out and maybe go down to my meditation room for some quiet time. As I quietly ease out of Russell's arms, he says softly, "Beautiful, you're so beautiful..." and seems to be dreaming peacefully.

I make my way quietly out the bedroom door and climb over Barney, who always sleeps right outside my bedroom. Come to think of it he usually barges in and wakes me up by bounding on the bed. It must be really early; Barney stretches and reluctantly follows me down the stairs. I find an old pair of shoes by the back door and slip them on, and then quietly open the back door and walk down to the meditation room. Barney loves coming in here, and after sprinkling in the flower bed, he runs down to me with excitement. I give him a big cuddle and then unlock the door.

The large meditation room is done out rather like a large log cabin, with a log fire, golden drapes, Buddha's, incense, candles and soft lighting dotted around. I put some logs on the fire, light some candles, some meditation incense and put on a meditation CD. Barney is lying flat out in front of the fire and I give him a quick belly rub and then make myself comfortable on one of the meditation chairs.

With my bare feet flat on the floor, I prepare to open myself fully to the spirit world:

Beloved, God, Jesus, Guardian Angles and Spirit Guides, I call you to me today and ask that you join me in

41

quiet contemplation time guiding and healing me in the way that you know is right and best for my higher being, thank you. I take a deep cleansing breath and then visualise roots growing down out of the soles of me feet, connecting me to mother earth and all its beautiful energies. Once I feel grounded, I visualise a beautiful golden cord running down from the top of my head, all the way down to my base chakra, allowing me to become centred and balanced. I then visualise myself stepping into a beautiful waterfall of rainbow colours, allowing the water to flow down my body, cleansing and replenishing me as it does so. Once refreshed, I visualise stepping from the water and placing a cloak of purple and gold around me to keep me safe and secure as I start my journey into the spiritual world.

I feel myself gently walking through a forest and approaching some steps. I walk up them slowly counting each step as I go, 1, 2, 3, 4, 5, 6, and 7. Upon reaching the top, I see a camp fire burning and make my way over to sit down next to it feeling the presence of Soul's strong powerful energy joining me instantly.

I sit and enjoy the powerful healing energy from the fire and Soul's presence for what seems like a long time before I quietly ask Soul, *What am I doing with Russell, Soul?*

Soul speaks to me softly, 'Beloved, the man that you leave sleeping in your bed is your soul mate. You have spent many life time's together and he is different from the other lovers you have experienced in the life you have now. You just need to let him in and learn to love men again.'

But what if he leaves me when he knows all of my truths?

'We know it can be difficult for you, a bit like living two lives in a way, but all of your truths and past learnings make you the good person you are today. A person who has developed a powerful healing connection to the divine. A person who has a good understanding of how people feel. A person who's past experience have taught her how

42

to be strong, responsible, intelligent, caring and capable. You are now a mature beautiful young woman with the capability and understanding to help so many human beings.'

That is such a beautiful thing to say to me. I always feel honoured in your presence.

'You know you have to learn through experience, but trust me when I say, let this man in, open your heart to him and you will be surprised. I protect you always and forever.'

I will try, Soul. Thank you.

I rise from my place of rest and make my way back down the steps that lead me to the forest, counting as I slowly walk back down 1, 2, 3, 4, 5, 6, and 7. Slowly, I walk back through the forest and find myself once again back within the meditation room. Slowly, I open my eyes and stretch. I give thanks and gratitude to God, Jesus, Guardian Angels and Spirit Guides for joining me on my journey this morning and for all the gifts, love, protect and healing that they give to me each and every day of my life. *Amen, God Bless.*

I make my way back up the stairs after cooking a hearty breakfast for the man lying in my bed. Barney races past me, barges through the bedroom door and jumps on the bed, waking Russell up. I can see Russell cuddle up to him and then open his eyes fully when Barney smothers him in a sloppy kiss. "As much as that's lovely old boy, I'd rather kiss your mistress," he says, making a right fuss of Barney. I can't help but laugh at the sight of the two of them. Russell sits up revealing his muscular chest and I can see light scratch marks on it from last night.

Russell seems to see what I'm looking at and smiles at me. "You can scratch me anytime, my love. That smells delicious I'm starving; breakfast in bed with a beautiful lady and a hairy mutt…what more could a man ask for."

She places the tray on my lap and pecks me on the cheek. "Actually, I'm heading for a shower, and then I thought we could take Barney to Runnymede Park and walk him through the forest. There's a great picnic area there once we've worn him out."

"I might skip breakfast and join you in the shower…it sounds more appealing."

"Maybe next time, wouldn't want your breakfast to get cold."

"Cold breakfast is fine by me if it means I get to share the shower with you."

"Eat your breakfast, Russell, you'll need your energy later for what I've got planned tonight." With that she winks and disappears into the en-suite for a shower.

I can't help but laugh at the cheekiness in her grin as she disappears. I haven't felt this happy in a long time.

"Do you need to drop by your place to get a change of clothes?" Penny asks as I come out of the shower.

"I have my gym bag in the car with clean shorts and T-shirt. I'll just change into those."

"OK great, I'll start packing up a picnic. Leigh-Anna will be in shortly to take us."

"I'll be down in a minute to help with the picnic once I'm dressed."

"I can manage," she says and turns to go out of the room.

As she turns I reach out to her and turn her around in my arms and kiss her softly saying: "I like to help you. In fact, I'd love it if you'd let me take care of you." With this she seems to go ridged in my arms.

"I can take care of myself. A man took care of me once and it didn't get me anywhere."

"I'm not that man, Penny, and that man must have been a complete idiot."

"I'll start on the picnic," she says wriggling out of my arms, and I'm left wondering who the arsehole is that seems to have mistreated her.

Leigh-Anna drops us off at the information area at

44

Runnymede Park, having told her that she'd ring her when we were ready to head home. I pick the picnic basket up and Penny glares at me, but I don't care, there is no way I'm allowing her to carry the basket on her own.

"If you're going to date me, then you will have to get used to me looking after you," I say firmly.

"Who said we are dating," she says back at me.

"Well, the fact that I slept in your bed all night after you seducing me kind of suggests we are dating, right?"

"It suggests nothing; in fact, it merely suggests that two consenting adults are having a bit of fun at the moment," she says walking off with Barney.

I practically have to run to catch her up. I take hold of her hand and turn her to face me: "Look, Penny, I don't know what has happened in your past and quite frankly I don't care. What I do care about is you; you're the most beautiful woman I've ever met, and I'd like to get to know you better."

"Let's just take this one day at a time and see where we go." Penny runs into the forest with Barney and shouts playfully, "Catch me if you can."

I chase after her laughing. *Oh where did they go?* I think to myself as they seem to have disappeared. "Barney!" I call out and sure enough he gives them away and rushes out from behind a big bush, charges towards me and knocks me flying, he then jumps on me and licks my face. I am covered in dog slobber.

Next thing I know, Penny is standing over me laughing. "Well, Mr Edwards, it would appear you have fallen over yet again…let me help you up." Grabbing both my hands, she pulls me into her and kisses me passionately.

Suddenly, she lets go and runs off again further into the woods. "Bet you can't catch me now!"

I get this game and I think to myself, *bet I can.* I laugh, following in her direction finding it hard to keep up with her, she finally starts to slow down. Finally, I catch up with her, pulling her to me this time I kiss her with longing.

"I slowed on purpose to give you more of a chance," she says.

"I was catching you anyway," I manage to say once I'd caught my breath.

"Yeah right…you where miles behind."

With that she takes my hand and we walk hand in hand through the forest until we come across a secluded area.

"I think Barney could do with a rest now; we have been walking for quite some time."

I lay the picnic rug out for her and take a bowl of water out for Barney, who laps it up thirstily. "We must have worn him out with all that running."

We settle down to our picnic, feeding each other the exotic fruits from inside the basket. The water from the melon drips down my fingers and she takes them into her mouth gentle sucking them suggestively whilst looking into my eyes. That's it, I'm gone again; my shorts are uncomfortable and I feel like I've been set alight. Barney starts to growl at someone that seems to be approaching us, snapping me out of my seductive thoughts.

"Mrs Chesterfield, well, fancy seeing you in this neck of the woods."

Penny's eyes turn frosted blue and she glares at the woman who is standing over us.

"Well aren't you going to introduce me to this hunk of a man?"

"The name's Miss West, not Mrs Chesterfield. Mr Edwards, this is Jennifer, an old acquaintance. Jennifer, this is Mr Edwards, who was a friend of mine."

Jennifer puts out her hand to me. "Nice to meet you," she purrs suggestively, holding on to my hand for longer than is necessary.

"Hello." I nod and sense Penny's unease with the woman. I shake my hand free of hers and take Penny's hand in mine, squeezing it gently. *I don't like this woman,* I think to myself. I can tell by her stance that she is no friend of Penny's and fancy talking to me in that manner when I'm clearly with someone. I hate that in a person.

The woman keeps eyeing me and I look away, still clinging to Penny's hand I start petting Barney, who still seems to be growling at this woman. He obviously doesn't like her either.

"Oh yes, I heard you went back to your maiden name after all that happened with William," the lady says.

"Well, if you'll excuse us, we are having a private conversation," Penny says harshly.

"I don't know if I'd be able to move on quite so quickly after what happened."

With that I think Penny is about to hit her as she gets up and gives the women a deadly stare. She starts to pack some of the picnic away and I get up to help her. "Well, life goes on. Where's William Junior?" Penny asks.

The woman seems to stumble her words in surprise at the question. "He's at home with his nanny."

"Oh, yes, the beautiful Mrs Chesterfield, how could I forget? Who are you here with anyway? Some other poor sod's husband?"

"Well, I might be, then I might not be."

"Goodbye, Jennifer. Have a nice life. Now, if you'll excuse me, I'm rather busy."

After an awkward silence Jennifer says: "It was lovely to meet you, Mr Edwards. Maybe I'll see you again sometime."

She leans towards me as if she is going to kiss me and I move backwards grabbing Penny and I say: "Well, just so you know, there's only one woman in the world for me, and she's standing right next to me." I kiss Penny passionately, hoping I give this Jennifer the hint. "Goodbye, Jennifer." With that she walks off without another word.

Penny looks at me and laughs: "I can't believe you just did that."

"Neither can I, but she needed to know where she stood. I'm a one woman kind of guy."

Penny settles herself back down and pours us both a big

glass of wine. "I could do with something stronger after seeing that bitch," she says and hands me a glass.

"I could tell she wasn't one of your favoured acquaintances. Penny, who is William?"

After a short pause Penny says, "William was my ex-husband, Russell. I am a widower."

"Oh, I'm sorry. I didn't know."

"Don't be sorry, how were you supposed to know?"

"So, who is William Junior?"

After a deep sigh Penny says, "William Junior is Jennifer and Williams's son, the son she fell pregnant with whilst he was married to me."

"Oh my God, Penny, how awful that must have been for you."

"At the time maybe, but I'm over it now." Penny kicks off her shoes and stands up, pushing her feet firmly into the grass beneath her, she turns her palms upwards and closes her eyes.

"So tell me about this William guy," I say standing next to her.

"Maybe someday, Russell, but for now, I'd like to just stand and centre myself after that encounter with Jennifer."

"OK, so how do we centre ourselves?" I ask wondering what she's doing.

"Well, kick of your shoes and socks and push your bare feet into the ground, and then visualise tree roots coming out of the soles of your feet. Next, turn your hands over, palms pointing upwards towards the sun." Softly, she takes both my hands and turns them over. "Ready, now visualise, sense a beautiful golden light coming in through the top of your head, and allow the light to stream all the way through your body, and then repeat after me: 'Safe, Centred, Balanced, Protected.' Then, enjoy the natural energy of mother earth coming up through the soles of your bare feet and the healing energy from the sun's natural rays entering your palms. Breathe in deeply through your nose and out through your mouth a few times, and allow your thoughts to take you wherever it is

48

you wish to go."

I don't know how long we stood there like that, but I do know that once Penny said, "I think we should make our way back now," I felt completely relaxed and at peace.

We packed away the picnic and made our way back to the information centre in silence, each of us lost in our own thoughts. Penny's driver was already there waiting for us. Once in the car I took her hand in mine and asked her if she was OK.

"Of course, I can't wait to get you home," she says smiling up at me.

I can't wait to get there either, I think to myself. And from the look in those eyes, I know she's going to take me again in the same passionate way she did the night before.

Sure enough, we were hardly through the door before she started stripping the clothes from my back and kissing me passionately, and I wondered if we would even be able to make it to the bedroom. *I can't wait to be inside this beautiful woman yet again. I just can't believe this is happening to me.*

"Couch will do just fine," she whispers seductively, pushing me down on to it, she takes me again just as she did the night before leaving me completely breathless.

===== *X* =====

Chapter Eight

I've been dating Penny for just over three months now, and whenever we're apart, I can't stop thinking about her. Having spent yet another brilliant weekend in her gorgeous company, I find myself struggling to concentrate on the boring reports laid out in front of me. She sure is a fascinating woman, I think, as I stare blankly at the workload on my desk. I pick up the phone, *shall I ring her? Maybe not,* I don't want to smother her too much; after all, I only left her house a few hours ago and she did say she was busy taking an art class today. I've managed to find out a few interesting facts about her, like she not only paints magnificent paintings, she also teaches students how to paint. She has told me herself that she lives two lives: one in this world painting, and one within the spiritual realms helping people find their true selves. Which is fine with me, I've seen for myself all the good that she does for people, and the charities her spiritual work helps, it's all very fascinating. If only I could get her to open up about William. I've tried to approach the subject on a few occasions but she just goes cold and walks away. That man has a lot to answer for I'm sure.

Now what was his name again? William Chesterfield, I find myself putting into my Google search. I probably shouldn't look him up but I can't help myself. That man has hurt the woman I love, and I need to know more about him. The fact that she is so loving one minute then distant the next can be confusing, not that it will make any difference to the way in which I feel about her. Oh yes, Penelope West, you have stolen my heart, and no matter what I will always love you.

Aha, now there he is…well, he sure was a good-looking man, although he does look arrogant with it. Who's that standing next to him? It can't be, but wait a minute, I'd know those eyes anywhere. She looks so different; curly hair, still stunning in her looks, but she

50

looks unhappy about something. She certainly doesn't look like the confident person that I know in fact her eyes look so sad, which breaks my heart. Looking at this picture I can tell that he's not my kind of person at all. The body language given off from Penny tells me this man didn't make her happy at all, the way he's possessively holding her, she looks completely uncomfortable with the picture that's been taken.

'Motor GP Rider dies after spending four weeks in intensive care following a freak accident at his last race in Brazil. Reports say that his mother and father were at his bedside when the life support machine was switched off, but there was no sign of his wife Penelope Chesterfield. This must have caused great devastation in the Chesterfield household after losing their other son Timothy six months ago when he took his own life by jumping in front of a train, leaving the Chesterfields with only one daughter.'

I don't think I can read anymore; I shouldn't have looked him up. How sad that one family could suffer such devastation in one year; maybe that's why Penny doesn't want to talk about it. After seeing that article, I can't resist, just the one small text, feeling slightly guilty that I'd pried into her past by looking up her ex-husband.

'Hi gorgeous, missing you already. Thanks for yet another great weekend. Hope you are well. Love you always and forever. Russell XX'

I keep looking at my phone in anticipation, hoping that she'll text me back, when Mrs Jones walks in holding my cup of coffee

My phone beeps and my heart jumps in excitement as there's a message from Penny.

'Of course I'm well, you only left me a few hours ago. Don't you have work to do? Lover boy. Always and forever, is a long time and time has a way of changing things. X.'

Lover Boy, honestly, I laugh to myself. But what does she mean by that last comment?

My phone rings making me jump.

"Russell Edwards."

"Mr Edwards, Grace is in reception and she wants to talk to you."

Oh not Grace, I suppose I should talk to her. I have been avoiding her since I caught her out.

"Oh, do I have to see her?" I say.

Suddenly, my door bursts open with Mrs Jones in tow saying, "You can't just burst in there like that."

"It's OK, Mrs Jones, I'll see her." *Let's get this over with.*

"Russell, you have been avoiding all my calls. I'm sorry to burst in like this but I needed to see you."

"I wonder why that might be, Grace," I say to her harshly.

"But, Russ, look, I'm so sorry I just wanted to see you to apologise and see if there is any way that you could find it in your heart to forgive me. I've been such a fool."

"You what! You not only sleep with someone else, but you also sleep with them in our bed. Grace, how could you? Then you have the balls to come here and expect me to forgive and forget. I don't think so somehow."

"It's because of her isn't it? You're with her now aren't you? I've seen you out with her, Russ."

"What do you expect me to do? Stay loyal to someone like you?"

"I don't know, I just thought maybe if we talked and worked things through, Russ, please."

"Stop calling me, Russ. I don't know what you expect from coming here today, but there is no way in the world that I would ever get back with you. I've sold the house I brought for us. It's over. You decided that the minute you climbed into bed with someone else. Just get out, now!"

"This isn't over, Russell. I'm going to make it up to you and win you back somehow."

"Get out now!" I have never felt so angry in my life;

52

I take the bottle of whisky out of my cupboard and pour myself a glass, draining it down in one, I then start to plough through the papers on my desk furiously. I had been working hard for quite some time when Mrs Jones gingerly brings me more coffee in. "Are you OK?" she asks.

"Yes, of course. The cheek of that woman." At least I've managed to get through most of the outstanding paperwork on my desk. Then my office door bursts open for the second time that day, but this time it's Penny, and she seems to be in a determined mood.

"Russell, quick, we must go and go now. It can't wait." She drags me out of my chair with urgency. "Leave all that. We must go now, we are needed. Have you been drinking? Don't worry, you can tell me about it on the way, once I've explained."

"What…on the way where? Where are we going? Wait, didn't you have an art class today?" I asked all confused at her sudden outburst.

"Some things are more important; now, come quickly, we have to get to the broads right now."

I get into Penny's Mercedes SLK and Penny steps on the gas, throwing me back in my seat. "Penny, what's going on? Slow down a bit."

"Russell, there's no time, we must get to your Mum straight away."

"What, why? What's happened?"

"Look, remember what I told you, sometimes I know when something is wrong."

"Yes, you told me over dinner once."

"Well this is one of those times; trust me, we need to reach your mother and at this point I'm not too sure why, but I know it is important. We must get to her quickly."

"But what about your art class and Barney? Surely, if my mother needs me she will call."

53

"Your phone will ring on our way. Rose is bringing Barney with her once she's cleared up the art room for me. I get the feeling we will need her."

I look at Penny confused. *Why all the rushing?* I don't quite understand what's going on here. Penny seems to be heading in the direction of the broads and is driving like a mad woman. She glances at me quickly then turns her focus back to the road. "Look, Russell, I know it's kind of hard to understand my spiritual work, but when Soul comes to me in the middle of an art class and tells me to get you and go to your mother and my aunt, I kind of know that something is wrong. I can feel it, I don't know how, but I just can, OK."

"A knowing without actually being shown, right. But please slow down, I don't want you getting pulled over and in trouble with the law."

"OK. So, do you want to tell me what's been going on for you today? Only you were as angry as hell when I arrived?"

"I had a visit from Grace. She wants to sort things out. Can you believe that woman?"

"Well, you have been avoiding talking things through with her."

"What's there to say. I am with you now and I'm not interested in anything she's got to say."

"That maybe so, but you still need to clear the air so that you can move on."

"There's no air to clear. I moved on the day I set eyes on you." My phone starts to ring in my pocket and I look at Penny: "How did you know? Hello, Russell Edwards." My father starts talking on the phone to me and I can't take in what he's saying. "What did you say, Dad?"

Penny puts her hand on my thigh and squeezes it reassuringly. "Everything's going to be OK, Russell, I know it is. Tell your father we will be there soon; we are maybe an hour away."

"Penny said we're about an hour away; we'll be there as soon as we can."

54

"But how come you're only an hour away?" Dad asks.

"I know, Dad, Penny came to get me out of work and we left over an hour ago."

"But the accident was around an hour ago. I haven't long arrived at the hospital."

"We'll be there as soon as we can, Dad."

"OK, son, I'll see you soon." My father's words choke over the phone and I know this is serious.

Penny glances at me quickly and squeezes my leg again saying: "Look, I know that everything is going to work out just fine, so try not to worry. She will be fine."

"What do you know? What did Soul tell you?"

"Just that Rose and I were needed and that your mother had an accident, but please remember that he also told me that everything would work out OK."

"Does that mean she will be fine?"

"Of course, if there's one thing I've learnt is that my spirit guide is always right and trustworthy. So try not to worry. Trust is something he's always telling me."

"OK, I'll try."

"It's hard I know, especially when life on earth deals you some hard blows."

An hour later we find ourselves walking through the entrance to the North Walsham Hospital. Penny squeezes my hand reassuringly as we approach the enquiry desk. After what seems an age the lady on reception points us in the direction of the intensive care unit. I can't believe it. I'm in a total daze. What kind of state are we going to find my mother in? All sorts of horrific thoughts are playing in my mind and it's as if Penny knows what I'm thinking.

"Hey, stop it, your mother is going to be fine. Remember, trust what I told you."

I just about manage to nod as I swallow the lump that's forming in my throat, and Megan comes bounding towards us crying her eyes out: "Oh, Penny, I'm so glad you're here."

"It's OK, Aunt Megan, just calm down everything is

going to be alright."

"We have to wait in the waiting room while they get Sylvia settled. I think the doctor is with her."

"What happened?"

"Well, we went into town, you know girls and their shopping. We had just come out of Roy's when this car came out of nowhere." She sobs in Penny's arms.

I see Penny drawing on her aunt's back and placing her hand over the place she had drawn and wonder what she's doing. But, whatever it was seems to have calmed her aunt down as the sobs seem to have eased, and then she shows us through to the waiting room and proceeds to tell us the rest of the story.

"It hit her and sent her flying. She summersaulted in the air, Pen. Oh God, please let her be OK."

My heart sank at those last words "summersaulted in the air". She's probably going to die. No.

Penny pointed to the chair next to her and as I slumped in it she whispered: "Trust." Placing her hand on my back I felt a soothing sense of warmth tingle through my spine. I look at her questioningly. "Go with it, Russell, it will help, OK." I nodded weakly. We seemed to be sitting huddled together; Penny with one hand on my back, the other on her aunt's. Finally, my father entered the room with a doctor in tow. As I looked at my father he suddenly looked like he'd aged and appeared to be very pale. I jump up and run to him, flinging my arms around him.

"She's OK, son, we can go in and see her."

"Now, Mrs Edwards has had quite an ordeal. We have put her into an induced coma for the next twenty-four hours to give her body time to recover, so things might look worse than what they really are," the doctor said as he led us to my mother's room.

Penny spoke to the doctor briefly asking if it was OK to do something or other, I couldn't quite take it all in. Whatever it was that Penny had asked seemed to please the doctor, as he nodded approvingly.

"Thank you, doctor for all you've done," Penny said as

we walked through the door.

"All in a day's work," the doctor smiled back. "Mrs Edwards will be fine. I'll leave her in your capable hands." He nods and then leaves us at the door.

There were tubes everywhere. I just froze with tears in my eyes, as I looked at my mother lying there helplessly. My father sat at my mother's bedside holding her hand, talking to her softly, telling her how much he loved her and that she was going to be alright. The whole scene in front of me just made me want to cry my eyes out, but I knew I had to stay strong for Dad. The question was how?

Penny turned to me and threw her arms around me, squeezing me really tightly, whispering in my ear: "You can do it, Russell. I know you can stay strong. I'm here with you and I'm going to help you through it. I'm going to give your mother all the healing I can while we're here, OK."

I nod. *How does that women know what I'm thinking or feeling?* I wonder. She leads me over to my mother's bedside and sits me down. "Just hold her hand and talk to her; she can hear you. Trust."

The next few hours pass in a blur; nurses and doctors coming and going, machine beeping, Penny drawing some kind of symbols in the air over areas around my mother's body, each time holding her hands in place for long periods of time, my father whispering sweet nothings, and Mrs West quietly watching from an armchair in the corner.

At some point during the day Rose arrived. Penny and Rose seem to be working endlessly on my mother's body, each time they change position, I'm sure I can see bright coloured lights moving around my mother's lifeless body…but what would I know. There's a gentle knock at the door and I think the nurse said something about a police officer wanting to talk with Megan. Penny touches my shoulder and kisses me slightly on the cheek saying,

"I'll be right back, Russell." I manage to nod at her as she leaves the room with Megan.

It seems like they've been gone ages and I feel so helpless just sitting here watching Rose and my father, who seems to have tears in his eyes. I've never seen him cry before; he's always been a strong man. *Where is Penny?* I want her back in here with me. My mother is just lying there looking dead. I feel my heart pounding. *Oh God, what can I do? Not my mother, please let her be OK,* is all that is going over in my mind.

Finally, Penny comes back into the room with a nurse. She locks eyes with me and whispers 'Trust'. The nurse tells us that all her vital signs are looking really good and that mother is responding well to the treatment that she's been given. My father is OK to stay the night, but she recommends that the rest of us go home and get some rest.

"How can I go home?" I manage to whisper.

Penny stands behind me and puts both her hands on my shoulders. "Russell, you look worn out. Please try not to worry; the hospital will call us if there is any change."

I don't remember going back to Penny's aunt's house or how I got into bed that night, I just remember waking next morning feeling completely exhausted. Barney lying closely by my side, he smells of fresh air as he gently nudges me with his big nose and stares at me with his sad looking brown eyes. "Barney," Penny says as she walks into the room holding a tray of coffee and croissants followed closely by Sky. "I thought he'd jump in my spot. How you feeling this morning?"

"Worn out. I don't remember getting home or into bed."

"I undressed you, Russell. You were so exhausted you just crashed on top of the bed. Eat your breakfast to keep your strength up, and then I'll take you to the hospital as soon as you're ready."

After a rushed breakfast and shower, I find myself being driven back to the hospital. As we approach the intensive care unit, the doctor who spoke to us yesterday approaches us.

"Aha, Mr Edwards, just the man I've been looking for." He leads us into the same side room we waited in yesterday and my stomach churns thinking *Oh God*, what must have happened? "Please don't look so worried, Mr Edwards, we will be waking your mother up in just a few moments. I wanted to ask, has you mother complained about any pains recently?"

"No, not that I'm aware of. Why, is there something wrong?"

"Like I just explained to your father, we have found that you mother has a heart murmur. Now, don't look so worried, it can easily be treated with medication. Just thought you should know that maybe this accident was some kind of blessing really. She could have had a major heart attack at any time. But now that we know we can prescribe her with the correct medication and we expect her to make a full recovery. We will be removing all her machines shortly so don't be surprised if you hear some bleeping, it's nothing to worry about. I'll show you to her room now if you're ready?"

"Thank you." Penny squeezes my hand as we follow the doctor to my mother's room. I don't know what I'd do without her.

My mother seems to be waking very slowly as I stand by my father's side watching and waiting. She starts to struggle with her mask and before I know it, Penny is pushing both my father and myself outside. I turn to see the heart monitor sound a low beep and a line appearing on the screen, as Penny quickly pushes me into the corridor and back into the side room. Penny pulls me into a big hug and whispers, "Russell, I know what you just saw then, but stay strong. I will be back shortly." My emotions are all over the place as I try to reassure my father that everything will be fine, whilst all the time in my own mind I really

59

don't know. After seeing the machine go out, I'm sure my mother must be dead.

A few hours later, after trying to get the attention of more than one nurse, Penny finally returns with the doctor. Penny smiles at me reassuringly and I immediately feel relieved. I can't quite make out what the doctor is saying, however, it appears that they have to leave my mother sedated for a few more days to allow her body more time to recover. So, we return back to the room once more, only to look at my mother's lifeless body.

===== *X* =====

Chapter Nine

The next few days pass in a blur with much the same routine; sitting at my mother's bedside by day, while Penny and Rose work their magic on my her body. Finally, when we arrive at the hospital on day three, they have woken my mother and she is in a side room on a private ward sitting happily, gazing into my father's relieved eyes.

I can't tell you the relief I felt as we approached my mother's bedside and kissed her.

"I've just told your mother that she's not allowed out of my sight in future...no more girlie shopping trips without me."

"Michael, don't be silly now, it was just a freak accident and I'm fine."

"You are now, my love, but it wasn't much fun sitting here watching you like that, not knowing what was going to happen. Fancy not telling me you were having chest pains I can't..."

My mother cut him off mid-sentence. "Now stop over-reacting. That is exactly why I didn't say anything, you're always fussing. I'm fine now and I will be shopping again."

"I must say, Mum, it's good to see your fighting spirit hasn't disappeared." I laugh.

"Don't encourage her," my father replies.

"Take your father for a cup of coffee before he drives me insane, Russell. I want to talk to this beautiful young lady of yours."

"I'm not leaving your side."

"Oh yes you are. You're making my blood pressure rise with all your constant fussing; besides, I wish to talk to Penny alone."

"Huh, I don't see why we can't stay, that woman is impossible sometimes," my father huffs as he follows me out the door. I can't help but laugh at the pair of them; what a difference a day makes, I think to myself as we leave the girls to chat.

"Well, Mrs Edwards, you gave us all quiet a scare. You really mustn't be so hard on Mr Edwards; he did look quite upset."

"He'll get over it; he always wants to know everything, nosy old git. Now, I needed to speak to you alone, only Megan has told me a few things about you and I need some clarification."

"Well, I hope it was all good things." I laugh at Russell's mother who looks so serious.

"Of course, my dear, and please call us by our Christian names; after all, we are practically family. I've seen the way Russell looks at you and the way you look at him. Reminds me of my courting days with Michael...so much love for each other. I'm hoping one day you'll be my daughter-in-law. Are you alright, dear, only you look a little pale?"

"Of course, you just took me by surprise is all. Your words are very kind, but Russell and I haven't known each other that long."

"Of course not, dear, but I'm an old romantic and I can see the love between you is something special. I knew it the first time we met, the way he looked at you. Ignore me, now where was I? I don't really know where to start?"

"The beginning is always good. I'm all ears."

"Well, it's like this, my dear. I went out shopping with a wonderful friend of mine only to be knocked down by something, and then my world went blank, I can tell you. Well, then all of a sudden, I was in this light tunnel travelling towards a light feeling completely peaceful." I pause to take a breath and then continue, hoping she will understand. "At the top of this tunnel was a closed gate and my daughter stood at the other side of the gate. Can you believe it...I've wanted to see her so much since she left?"

"Oh, Sylvia, how wonderful," I say to her while she lay crying in my arms. "Did she talk with you?"

"Yes, she gave me the biggest cuddle a mother could wish for and said, 'I can't open the gate for you as it's not your time yet. Please understand. I'm sorry. I love you and talk to Penny about awakening. You must return now, I'll come for you when it's time for you to join me.'

The next thing I remember there was a very loud bang, then on and off different bright stars, like lights, of all different colours coming and going, then I'm awake in this bed and everyone is here. Can you please explain this all to me?"

I hold Sylvia in my arms for quite some time until the tears subsided. "Sylvia, you had an out of body experience."

"Megan has told me you do spiritual work."

"Yes, I'm a medium, I connect to peoples loved ones in spirit and give messages to them."

"You are psychic."

"Well, yes, we are all psychic; people confuse mediumship with being psychic all the time."

"What do you mean? Can you please explain all this to me?"

"Of course; I'd be delighted to. Being psychic simple means learning to listen to your own gut instinct. You know that feeling in your stomach when you go to do something and it ties up in knots usually means it will go wrong, then the feeling of fluttering butterflies when something feels right usually means what your doing will work out well. Being a medium is when we connect directly to our loved ones and guides in the spirit world, something we can all learn to do. Through developing our psychic abilities by using methods such as meditation, stillness, quiet contemplation, walks in nature and focus, we can all learn to connect to our own spiritual energy or body if you like, and then connect to our loved ones, guides and helpers from the spiritual realm."

After a long pause Sylvia said, "Will you teach me? And what is awakening?"

I couldn't help but smile: "Your daughter has obviously seen me help Rose with her awakening group. It's simply a group that we made up to help people like yourself to learn how to connect to their own energy and the energy of their loved ones."

"How wonderful; what do I have to do? Can I join?"

The boys return to the room as I give her my answer. "Of course, I have the perfect idea. Just get better first."

"The perfect idea for what?" the boys say together.

"Never you mind…it's girlie talk," Sylvia says.

"Russell, I need to go and see an old friend in Cromer. I'll be back to pick you up later."

"OK, darling, don't be too long," he says, kissing my cheek and looking at me questioningly. I know he knows I'm up to something; maybe I'll tell him later or maybe I'll leave him guessing.

It's been ages since I've been to the shop I bought in Cromer and left Dawn to run; of course, I check in with how things are going every week and she rings me with any queries. So, it's not surprising when she seems both delighted and surprised by my entrance.

"Penny, hello, how are you? It's been ages."

"Hi, Dawn, how's it all going?"

"Really great. I've sold an amethyst cathedral this morning and I have just finished my last treatment for the day. What about your end? Is there something I can get for you?"

"Yeah, it's all going great and since you asked, I need you to set up an awakening group for me."

"Awakening group? I know how to run circles, and shares etc., but I don't think I've heard of an awakening group."

"That's probably because it's something Rose and I made up."

"Really? Now I am intrigued. Tell me all."

"It's a group we set up to help individuals learn how to connect to their own spiritual energy without fear. You know sometimes people can become frightened of their own shadow when it comes to spirituality. So, we invented a group specially to help people connect to their own spiritual energy without the fear that sometimes we can instil within ourselves. It will be a simple group, starting with quiet meditation followed by some healing and then discussions."

"I'm all for that, tell me more."

I proceeded to explain to Dawn what my idea was and that I already had someone lined up for the group, which of course would only be small to start with. After reassuring her that Rose and I would start the group for her and then leave her to run it, she seemed more than happy to be part of it.

"Tell me when we can get started? After what you've explained, I can think of a few clients that would be more than happy to join us."

"Great, it will probably be in a few weeks' times. I need to clear things with Rose and allow the lady I have in mind a few weeks of recovery time before we get started. I'll ring you with a date once I know."

"Excellent, can't wait."

Sylvia has been out of hospital now for just over a week and is making good progress. After tying up some loose ends, I make my way to Mystic Pen's shop in Cromer where we will start our first awakening group. Russell seems to be fidgeting next to me. I've told him he doesn't have to go, but he insisted on supporting the group I've set up for his Mum.

"You know you don't have to join in, Russell."

"But I want to, and I want to support what you're doing."

"OK, darling, but quit fidgeting, it's driving me mad. I'm not going to kill you."

"I know you'd never do anything to hurt me and that's one of the many things I love about you."

"If it makes you nervous then just watch in the sidelines, OK."

"Fine, but I'd like to know more."

"I'm not here to convince you about anything…you supporting what I do is enough."

When we arrive at the shop, we find that Dawn has already set up the room above with gentle music. Incense and candles are burning, with chairs set out around the room in a circle occupied by friendly looking people chatting away amongst themselves. The atmosphere is just right and I can feel the presence of spirits all around me.

"Hi, Dawn, the room looks fantastic."

"Glad you like it; everyone is here already, and I can't wait to get started."

"Good evening, everyone. My name is Penny and this is my good friend Rose. We are here this evening to help you connect to your own energy and the energy of your loved ones within the spirit world without fear. For most of the time, fear is created by our own negative thoughts and the thoughts that we need to do things a certain way. Know that you are a human being with a spiritual energy that is beautiful in every way. You have nothing to fear; your spiritual body or soul, if you prefer, only sees everything through love. There is no right or wrong way on this journey, and everyone's journey is unique to them. Spirit will work with you at your own pace and if you work from the heart with love, light and good intensions, your loved ones will be more than happy to help. There is nothing to fear. Our loved ones in spirit want to help us on our journey in all that we do; they are often close by, but never interfere with our own free will. A good starting point is to learn to connect to our own spiritual energy and then progress with connecting to the energies around us, which is what this group is all about."

I was pleased to see that Russell had taken a seat next to his mother and seemed to be feeling more relaxed than he did on the journey here. The atmosphere within the room seemed to have a calming effect on everyone within the small group, so I hope that the group would continue once I was back home.

"We start the group this evening with a short opening prayer, so I ask that you join me in closing your eyes for a few moments.

"'Beloved Spirit, we invite you to join us here this evening in quiet contemplation. Help us to bring the two worlds closer together and assist us in the work that we do here tonight. We ask that you bring healing, peace and love to those in this room and the world that need it the most. Thank you. Amen.'

"Sometimes it can be hard to focus to begin with when doing meditation, thoughts of everyday life will come to you, which is OK, so acknowledge them and then bring your focus back to your meditation. When I started on this journey, I found the easiest way was to simply say the word *focus* and then focus on a pillar candle. You will learn what works for you as your own journey progresses.

"I'd like you to gently close your eyes, focus on my voice and take three very deep breaths, breathing in through the nose and out through the mouth. Now, imagine, sense or feel yourself lying in a meadow, and above you, is a perfect clear blue sky and the sun's rays are shining down over your body. You are completely at peace.

"Imagine yourself lying for a few moments in this tranquil place; it's a beautiful day, you are completely safe and no harm can come to you as the sun's rays bring healing throughout your entire body. Whilst lying peacefully within this meadow you can hear the gentle sway of the trees within the distance and the birds singing merrily within the trees. As you lie peacefully within these surroundings know that you are also a spiritual being and as you become more aware of this magnificent world you now exist in, you become lighter and safer with every breath that you take.

"I'd like you to gently rise from your place of rest and as you take a look around you, become aware of a path through the meadow which leads directly through to some trees and then take a few moments to view your surroundings."

I allow the group a few moments to take in their surroundings before continuing with the meditation, and I am quietly pleased that Russell is joining in with the group. This could be a good experience for him. It's nice to be with someone who shows an interest in what I do.

"Slowly you begin to walk along the path, feeling safe and secure you continue to the entrance of the forest. In front of you is a gate, you open this gate and walk straight through it. You find yourself within the centre of a forest and in front of you are seven steps leading upwards towards a beautiful blossom tree. These steps lead directly to your guardian angel. You feel completely safe and secure as you begin to climb the steps.

"Step 1, you feel completely calm and relaxed; Step 2, you feel at peace within yourself; Step 3, you take your time, there is no rush; Step 4, there is no fear, you are completely safe; Step 5, you begin to feel very light; Step 6, you're almost there and you can see a bench underneath the tree with beautiful blossom falling all around it. Step 7, you stand for a moment and take in your surroundings. How do you feel within yourself? Take a good look around you, and remember what you see. How do you feel? This is who you really are. You take a few steps towards the bench and allow yourself to rest quietly there. As you rest quietly on this bench the blossom falls gently around you and birds sing in the distance, and you begin to feel the presence of your guardian angel who takes a seat next to you. I leave you for a while with your guardian angel; talk to them freely about your feelings and know that they will listen without judgement."

The group sits quietly this way for ten minutes before Rose suggests bringing them back to the room.

"You give your guardian angel a hug and thank them for their presence, as they wrap their wings around you, you send them your love. It is time for you to return; as you stand you watch as they disappear from you, and then standing, you make your way back towards the steps. You begin to make your way back down the steps: 7, 6, 5, 4, 3, 2, 1. You make your way back towards the gate and open it and you find yourself lying back within the meadow. Gradually, feel yourself back within this room, when you are ready open your eyes."

We spend some time after the meditation discussing how it made everyone feel and what they saw on their journey. Rose and I answered any questions that were thrown at us before sitting everyone in pairs and assisting the group giving healing to each other. Most of the group were slightly unsure as they hadn't done healing of any kind before. As Rose explained, it's all about your intension, just allow spirit to work with you in love and light and state that you intend to give healing to the person sitting before you and then listen to the guidance of spirit. Everyone seemed to be completely relaxed by the end of the evening as we finished with a closing pray.

"'Beloved Spirit, it is with much love and gratitude that we thank you for your love and presence here this evening. Thank you for bringing this group together and for working with us this evening. We thank you for all the healing and support that you give to us each and every day as we make our journey on the earth plain. God Bless to you all. Amen.'"

After leaving Dawn with all the different meditations that we'd put together for the group, Russell and I make our way back home.

"Thank you for a lovely evening, Penny. Oh, by the way, I almost forgot...mother wants us to take Megan round for dinner tomorrow evening."

"Are you sure she's up to it now, Russell? She hasn't long been out of hospital."

"She told me she's hired someone to do the hard work and wants to have you over after everything you've done to help."

"Well, OK. If you're sure she's up to it, but then I

really must get back to my art classes."
  "OK, darling."

===== *X* =====

Chapter Ten

Penny, Megan and I made our way round to my parents' house and I noticed that mother had borrowed Megan's friend, Florrie, to help with all the cooking. The table looked fantastic laid out with my mother's best fine china and crystal glasses. Fancy napkins were all fanned neatly, with candles burning in the centre of the table just for effect.

"Well, Penny, you finally brought Russell round so that I can show him what I've been up to with the renovations. I don't know, since he's met you he spends all his time with you. Young love hey, dear."

My father seems intent on teasing us this evening I notice.

"Take no notice of him, dear, and come and take a seat. I've sat you next to Michael with Russell opposite and I hope that's OK. Although I may have to alter the seating arrangements, Michael, if you are going to tease the young lovers all evening."

"Tease me, never. I think it's great; I haven't seen our son this happy before."

"That's absolutely fine by me. After all, if Russell is opposite me, we can play footsie all evening," Penny says while caressing my leg underneath the table.

"I can't believe you just encouraged them," I said smiling.

"Me, encourage them, never," Penny quoted innocently.

Yeah right, like she's the innocent one here; she's forgetting I'm on the receiving end of her foot caressing my leg, and if she doesn't stop soon, I'm going to be extremely uncomfortable all evening with my growing erection. Strange, I thought, *when you first meet someone and begin to form that sexual relationship you seem to be at it like rabbits, but then the feelings slow down a bit. But not with Penny...that woman has me at my knees. I wouldn't have it any other way.*

"Russell, are you listening to me?"

"Sorry, father, I was miles away."

"I'm starting to think you two are really playing footsie under this table."

"Wouldn't you like to know?" Penny laughs then strokes my cock with her toe.

I might have to skip dinner and take Penny upstairs if she carries on with this torture.

"I was telling you about the boat I purchased."

"I remember now; you did say something about getting a boat."

"Well Jack, Florrie's husband, he knew someone up river who was selling one."

"Have you taken it out yet?"

"There's a few minor repairs Jack is helping with first; I'll show you after dinner."

"Great."

Florrie brought starters in and my father proceeded to tell Penny and me all about his new boat and the renovations he'd been making on the house. Apparently, Jack was quite the handyman who could turn his skills to almost anything. He was even building them a wooden summerhouse in the garden, which would overlook the river.

My father's topic of conversation changed during the main course when he decided it would be a good idea to talk about me as a child. Funny, I thought that was something only mothers did, embarrass their children in front of their future wives. Did I just say wife? Yes, well I could quite easily see myself married to Penny with a few children running around us. Funny how time changes...the thought of it all a few months ago with Grace had filled me with dread, but now with Penny it is so different. I couldn't imagine my life without her, despite the mystery of William still left to solve.

"So you see, Penny, Russell has done us proud over the years, finishing college and university with top grades, then stepping into my shoes at the solicitors, taking over when I'd had enough. There's only one thing left for him to do now."

"Oh, and what might that be?"

"Well, settle down of course, dear."

Something about Penny changed the moment my Dad spoke those words. I knew something was wrong, but I didn't know what. She had gone very pale, quiet and was picking at the dessert in front of her. How I wished she'd open up to me about her past; I'm sure it has something to do with her ex in some way.

"Penny, was everything alright with your dessert?" my mother asks.

"Oh, its fine, Sylvia, but I can't eat another bite I'm afraid."

"It's not like you to miss dessert, Pen. Are you feeling OK?" her aunt asks looking concerned.

"I think maybe I need some fresh air if you wouldn't mind. Please excuse me."

"I'll come with you. I could do with some air myself."

"I'll join you in a few minutes once my dinner's gone down…maybe show you that boat," my father shouts after us.

I wrap my arm around Penny as I lead her down the garden towards the edge of the river.

"Are you cold?" I ask as she shivers.

"Maybe a little."

"Here, have my jacket." I'm sure I see tears in her eyes as I wrap my jacket around her and pull her to me. This is not the lady I know.

"Take no notice of what father says, Penny. He can be old-fashioned at times."

"It's not your father, Russell. Your father is like you, a wonderful man. I've never met someone like you before who wants to look out for me and support the things I do, but…"

"But what, Penny? I want to take care of you and spend the rest of my life with you. No buts, just you and me together, forever. I love you, Penny, from the minute our eyes met I knew there was something between us. Can't you feel it, the chemistry we have. The way you make me feel is like nothing I've ever felt before and I'd move heaven and earth for you. That's how strong my love is for you. I never want us to be apart."

"I do love you, Russell, but there are things I can't give to you."

"There's nothing you can't give to me, Penny. I love you with all my heart."

"Ah, there you both are. Are you feeling better, dear, only I was going to show you round this boat of mine. That's if you feel up to it?"

"Sure, why not."

"Are you sure? I could just tell my father we'll see it another time," I whisper softly to her.

"We wouldn't want to spoil his excitement."

I wish I knew what was bothering her. My father sure has good timing sometimes.

We followed my father over to his boat.

"I'm going to rename it Suzie after your sister, but don't tell your mother that yet, it's a surprise."

"What a wonderful idea," Penny says.

Penny seems over-enthusiastic as my father shows us around his new boat, completely oblivious to Penny's distress. But she doesn't fool me. I may not have known her for years and years, but I've known her long enough to know that something my father said over dinner is distressing her.

"When you two finally get married and give me lots of grandchildren, I can take them out on the boat with me and teach them all about the river. A grandson first would be wonderful as we need another Edwards to carry the family name on. But of course we can't decide the sex of our children. Shame really, but that's the way these things work."

"Are you alright, dear, only you don't look to good at all. Maybe you need to lay down for a while."

Penny's face had turned completely pale and her eyes were full of tears.

"I think I best take you home, darling."

"No, here, I'll be fine, you stay here tonight and I'll see you tomorrow or something."

Before I know it Penny had passed my jacket back to me and quickly made her way back to the house.

"Penny, wait, what's wrong, love? Hang on a minute."

"What did I say?"

I ran straight through the house and passed my confused mother who called after me, "What happened? Penny just run straight out the front door."

"Not now, mother."

Finally, I caught up with her at her aunt's front door fumbling about for her keys.

"Penny, hey are you crying. Come here. What's wrong? We can sort this out."

"No we can't, Russell, I'm no good for you."

"What, where did that come from? You're everything to me."

"No I'm not, just leave, Russell, we can't do this anymore. We weren't meant to fall in love. This was just meant to be some fun between two consenting adults."

"I'm not going anywhere; I love you, Penny, so tell me why it's so wrong to fall in love."

She turned to face me with tears streaming down her face. This is not the strong woman I know. She reminds me of the sad lady in the article report I'd looked up. The one she was photographed in with William. *He is making my blood boil now.*

"We can sort this out, just talk to me."

Penny was silent in my arms and I couldn't bear it anymore, so I just bellowed the first thing that came into my head. She had to know I wasn't like him. Surely she knew that.

"I'm not him! I love you with all my heart!"

"I can't give you what you need. What is expected of you? You can't love me. You must go now before we get even more hurt."

"I don't think so; I'm not going anywhere. We belong together; where you go, I go, no matter what. Just tell me and I'll sort it. Whatever it is, whatever it takes."

"This is not some fairy tale, where happily ever after happens…this is real life. I've tried not to let this happen. I've tried not to fall in love with you but…"

"But what? I don't understand? I love you and you love me, so what else do we need?"

"Marriage means children, Russell. Like your father says, 'someone to carry on the family name'."

"I don't quite follow? Yes marriage, children…well, that all comes later when we're ready, no need to hurry. We have all the time in the world."

"You don't understand; I always swore I'd never marry again."

"I'm not him. You can't walk away from me, Penny. I thought you just said you loved me. What did he do to you? Please, help me to understand?"

"It's all for love that I let you go, Russell. I can't come between you and your family of what is expected of you in the future. You see you can't help me, no one can. I can't have children, Russell. I'm infertile."

With that Penny turns around and walks into her aunt's house, closing the door behind her and leaving me speechless on the front doorstep.

I can't believe what just happened, I think to myself as I stare at the door that has just been closed on me. I'm struggling to make sense of it all as I slowly turn to make my way back to my parents' house. In a bit of a daze, I stand for a while. *Should I go back and talk to her?* How did things go so wrong? One minute we were sitting at my parents' house enjoying a pleasant evening and then the next, all hell broke loose? *What do I do now?*

Desperately trying to make sense of our last conversation, I begin to remember the last few words that Penny spoke to me: 'It's all for love that I let you go, Russell. I can't come between you and your family of what is expected of you in the future.' Yes, that was her exact words. Maybe I should go back and knock on the door and make her talk to me about William.

I turn back again and make my way back to the door, lifting my hand ready to knock the door down if necessary. I suddenly stop mid-air thinking, *Oh God, what did she say?* 'You can't help me, no one can. I can't have children, Russell. I'm infertile.' Where does that leave us in the future? Maybe I need some time to digest this new information. But she said she loved me and I know for sure that I love her. Could I live my life without children, now that's a good question? I don't understand…why did she not tell me all this before?

'I'm not good for you. We weren't meant to fall in love. This was just meant to be some fun between two consenting adults.' Penny's words ring in my ears as I remember parts of the conversation.

With a heavy heart I turn around and slowly make my way back round to my parents' house, not quite knowing what to make of everything. Maybe we need a night apart just to think things through and then I could try talking to her tomorrow.

===== X =====

Chapter Eleven

Frantically, I dial Rose's number yet again for the umpteenth time. I can't focus on anything anymore; my mind is all over the place. Where is she? Has someone got her? What is she doing now? Will that blasted woman answer her damn phone?

"Russell, hi, what can I do for you?"

"Any news?"

"Not as of yet, but…"

"No one can just disappear off the face of the earth, Rose. Where is she?"

"She needs time, Russell; she will be back."

"Time, it's been two weeks. No trace of her anywhere."

"I know it's hard for you, but you need to be pat—"

"Please don't say that word again, Rose, it doesn't help. I'm dying here. Did Leigh-Anna show you the threatening letters?"

"Yes, I've seen the letters."

"Well!"

"Well she will be back, when she's ready."

"How can you be so sure? She could have been abducted by some maniac."

"So, she has an admirer."

"Some maniac you mean; she could be dead for all we know."

"Don't be so melodramatic, Russell. I know you're stressed but…"

"But nothing, Rose, I need her back. I need to talk to her."

"I know you do, my dear, and you will talk to her. You were meant to be together, I've to…"

"Yeah, Yeah, I know you've told me it all before. She'll come back and we'll live happily ever after. Right now it doesn't feel that way."

"Time is all she needs. She is safe, I know in my heart that she is. She just needs some space to think."

"If you hear anything from her, anything at all, you'll call me straight away?"

"Off course, off course. And, Russell, try not to worry; she'll be back soon, I can feel it."

I can't believe I've been such a fool. Why didn't I knock that door down, when she closed it on me? But oh no, I just stood there dumbfounded by the revelation that she couldn't have children. So yeah right I was stunned but instead of trying to talk to her, I walked away. How am I going to fix this? It doesn't matter to me that she can't have children. Yeah, so I always thought that one day I'd have children but that changed the minute I fell in love with someone who couldn't have any. What must she have felt when William fathered a child with that awful Jennifer woman.

How did it all go so wrong? One minute we're playing footsie under the table over a nice meal with my parent and her aunt, the next I'm here wondering where the hell she is and how in the hell am I going to fix this mess. There has to be a way, I can't live my life without her now. God, I hope she's alright. I'm such a stupid arse sometimes.

I know it's only five o'clock but I'll just take one last stroll through the forest before I head home. Now that I've had time to think, I feel much better about the whole Russell business and know that I've done the right thing. Yeah, so I know that I'll miss his handsome face and loving arms, but I can't come between him and his family. Yes, I've definitely made the right choice. My heart will heal eventually and so will his when he meets the right lady who can give him what is expected of him.

I take a deep breath; there's nothing like the smell of dew early in the morning. I love being in nature, birds singing, trees swaying…it's so peaceful. What a beautiful place this is, I must remember to bring Barney here next time I come. I hope he's alright; of course, I will probably have to put him on a diet when I get back. Knowing Megan, she's fed him all sorts of left overs and spoilt him rotten.

As I walk further into the forest I start to feel slightly uneasy. If I didn't know better, I'd say someone was following me. What was that sound? Don't be silly, Pen, probably just some wild animal running through the trees. I clearly see Soul standing in front of me and as I'm about to acknowledge his presence, my world falls into darkness.

Chapter Twelve

I wake with a start. I'm perspiring and breathing really quickly. As I take my time to fully awaken myself, I realise that I'm in my own bed, in my own bedroom, covered from head to foot in sweat from the nightmare that abruptly woke me up. What a night. I know I haven't been sleeping too well since Penny left, but that dream was something else. It seemed so real, but then I guess dreams sometimes do seem a little weird, I shrug to myself as I rise from my pit.

I glance at the clock: 5.30am. God, it's early but phew, I stink, time for a shower. Yes, that should wash away the dreadful thoughts that a nightmare like that can bring to mind. I check my phone as I wait for the shower to warm up. There's no messages from Rose or Penny, much to my disappointment; still, no news is good news, so they say. I stand under the shower and wash away the loneliness I've felt since Penny left. Only it doesn't make me feel any better and the more I think about the dream, the more uneasy I feel.

I quickly dry and dress, I'm not being fobbed off anymore. Today's the day I get my girl back, with or without anyone's help. I feel a new sense of determination as I head out the door. First stop Rose's, to explain that dream. That dream may have been nonsense but it seemed real to me, and the more I think about it the more I feel afraid for the woman who's stolen my heart. I speed out the driveway and on to the main road with suddenly a strong urge to head to Penny's place. OK, Penny's place it is then.

As I pull into Penny's driveway, I see lights on in the house and a police car parked out front. What is going on? I storm up to the front door and as I'm about to knock, Leigh-Anna flings the door open and almost knocks me flying.

"Russell, hi sorry, no time to talk, I've got to get the car out. Rose is inside with Chris. He can explain all but try not to disturb Rose though, as we need her connected if we're to find this place." Before I can answer she's gone. What the hell is going on? Who is Chris? Well I guess there's only one way to find out. I stomp inside only to be greeted by lots of commotion.

"What is going on?" I bellow above the noise.

"And who might you be?" A rather thick set bodybuilder type greets me, in a rather intimidating way. But I'm not in the mood to be intimidated today.

"I could ask you the same question. What are you doing in this house?"

"What are you doing in this house?"

"Look this is getting us nowhere. Where is Rose?"

"Who's asking?"

"Chris, it's fine, this is Russell. Russell meet Chris. Chris meet Russell."

"Rose, what the hell is going on? I wake up this morning early after some kind of nightmare, I shower then have a really strong urge to come here and I find all this. Where is Penny, Rose? Can someone please tell me what is going on?"

"I'm sorry, mate, I didn't realise who you were. I'm Leigh-Anna's brother Chris, and we kind of have an emergency going on here."

"I can see that…"

"Russell, a nightmare you say," Rose interrupts us.

"Yes, but you're scaring me now, Rose. Is Penny alright?"

"Tell me about your nightmare, Russell. You see, I was woken about five o'clock this morning with this feeling. It's not good, we need to get on the road and find her, Russell. I've tuned into my guides and I know she's alive, but someone has her, I can feel it."

"Oh my God, it's the dream isn't it?" I feel sick.

"Do you need to sit down, Russell? You're awfully pale. Tell me about this dream and try not to worry, I've found people before, Russell. With Chris and Leigh-

Anna's help, I will find Penny, trust me, I will."

"What are we waiting for, let's go."

"Not so fast. When I get on that road I need to concentrate on my route. Your dream, Russell, it may be significant."

"Well, I don't know. I was in a forest somewhere watching as this man placed what looked like a white cloth over a lady's mouth; she fell against him, and he dragged her away from me. As I woke, all I could think of was Penny."

"A forest you say? I knew there were trees around her. What kind of forest, Russell?"

"Well, there was this one time when I went to the new forest as a child and stayed somewhere amongst the trees, it was a peaceful place from what I ..."

"Russell, you are a darling," Rose says as she kisses me. "Has Leigh-Anna got the car, the new forest is where we are heading, Chris, there's no time to waste."

"How do you know that's where we have to go?"

"There is a reason for everything, Russell, and a reason you were brought here today. Now, are you coming or not?"

"Leigh-Anna, where's the car?"

"I remember Stan taking it for a service yesterday, but I thought he was bringing it back last night. It's not in the garage though, perhaps there was a problem."

"Here, let's take mine."

"Is it OK if Chris drives, Russell? Only he's helped me with these sort of things before."

"Sure, now let's go get my girl!"

Chris takes the driver's seat and Rose takes the seat next to him with myself and Leigh-Anna in the back, and as we pull out on to the main road, I notice the police car that was parked outside Penny's following behind us. Rose is rubbing her temples and with her eyes closed she tells Chris to head for the motorway, saying something about following the exact route that Penny had taken two weeks ago would help to trace her movements.

We have been travelling so far along the M25 when Rose tells Chris to pull into the next service station. When we come to a stop, Rose gets out of the car and looks all around before getting back in and saying, "Yes, this is the same route, continue on the M25 a few more miles. She stopped here for fuel."

We seem to be flying along the M25 at a great speed and I can't help thanking the police escort that we seem to have as I'm sure we'd have been pulled over for speeding miles back. I look over at Leigh-Anna and we half-heartedly smile at one another. Chris certainly knows how to drive at high speed and I can't help but wonder what he actually does for a living.

"Pull onto the M3, Chris. Follow this until the M27, there is a service station somewhere along here where we need to stop. Yes, this is the road, keep going." Rose seems to be in some kind of trance as she keeps bellowing instructions along the way to Chris, who nods in obedience and drives with expertise.

We pull into some kind of service station just before the M27, and Rose gets out once again. "She was here. Her car is here."

"What? Her car is here, where?"

"Patience, Russell, let Rose concentrate," Leigh-Anna scolds me.

"The Travel Lodge. She stayed in the Travel Lodge overnight, then hired a car from here."

"Why would she stay in a Travel Lodge, then hire a car?"

"She wanted time alone to think, Russell. She didn't want you following her; she wanted to be on her own, with her own thoughts."

My heart sinks as Rose's words hit home: *why did I let her go?*

We check with the Travel Lodge and sure enough a Penelope West had stayed there two weeks prior to our arrival. Next, we check out the car hire company attached to the Travel Lodge who only confirm that she hired a vehicle after Chris rather forcefully shows them some kind of identification badge. I don't think I'd want to get on the wrong side of him somehow, but I can't see how all this is helping.

We find Penny's car in the parking lot and Chris breaks into it while the police escort turns the other way, although there didn't seem much point as we still have no leads as to where she went. At least I have her scent, I think to myself as I pull Penny's cardigan to my face and breathe in. I found it in the back of her car…not that it's going to help us find her.

Eventually, after travelling what seems like an age, we turn onto the A31.

"Head for Brockenhurst," Rose tells Chris, who nods compliantly.

I know she's concentrating but I can't help asking; after all, we have been travelling an awful long time and anything could have happened in the time that's past. "Rose, I don't mean to interrupt your trail of thought but is she still alive and well?" I choke out.

"Yes, Russell. I feel she is very much alive and very much aware of her surroundings. She has a spirit child with her who will lead her out of the hut she is in."

===== X =====

Chapter Thirteen

I wake suddenly with a fuzzy head and try to move my arms but they are tied behind my back. Where am I? My mouth is as dry as a desert rat's arse, whatever that might be. Now, Penny, no time for jokes, time to try and think clearly. Right, so you're sitting in a chair with your hands tied around the back of it and your feet are tied at the ankles. God, what I wouldn't give to stretch out right now in my own bed snuggled up to Russell and Barney.

I take a look around this make-shift hut, which looks to me something like a child has built and notice a small spirit child sitting in the corner watching me. I can hear what sounds like someone chopping outside and shiver with the cold and fear of who it is and what my fate maybe, when suddenly the spirit child speaks: 'He's out chopping wood; he won't harm you. He's obsessed with you and will do anything for you. He thinks by bringing you here he can make you fall in love with him. I have a plan though.'

I take a few moments to clear my fuzzy head before I'm able to answer with my thoughts. 'So, what's this plan of yours?'

'Well when he returns, you're to make out that you're really hungry. He wants to keep you happy see, so he will go off to get you some food and then we can make a run for it. I'll lead you safely out of here and back through the forest to the dirt track.'

'Right, and how do you suppose I break out of this tape which is keeping my hands and legs bound?'

'Easy, the tape holding your wrists together can be cut through using the nail that is sticking out at the back of the chair.'

It takes me a few moments to take in what the spirit child has told me then suddenly I try to feel around the back of the chair for the nail. Finally, I manage to get a feel for where the nail is and start to move my hands up and down in the hope that it will cut through the tape. *Steady, don't cut yourself, he will be back in any minute.* Sure enough this rather vulgar looking man opens the door, and the draught from outside makes me shiver.

"Good, you're awake, I was starting to worry. You're shivering, here…I'll wrap this blanket around you and then get the fire going. That should warm you up."

'Remember what I told you; this man is smitten with you. Keep him talking and then ask for some food. Tell him you're starving, he wants to please you.'

I clear my throat before speaking. "Hi, what's your name?"

"I uh, I'm not sure if that's really relevant."

"Of course it's relevant, if you're to be my new friend we should at least know each other's names."

'You're doing great, that's it; be his friend.'

"Friend, uh, well I was kind of hoping for more. Wait a minute, you're not still with that soppy boyfriend are you?"

"How do you…"

"I've seen him. I've watched him come and go. I've seen the two of you together."

"Well, if you've been watching you will have noticed he hasn't been around for the last few weeks."

"I wondered about that. Yeah, why are you here on your own? Why wasn't he with you?"

"We broke up."

"That's great, so we can be together then."

"Yes, well I guess we could, but wouldn't it be easier to untie me then we could talk properly like real friends."

"I'm not sure. How do I know you won't run out on me?"

"Well, as friends we need to trust each other."

"Let me get this fire going then maybe, I don't know, we'll see."

"You could at least tell me your name…that would be a start. I'm Penny."

"I know who you are. I know everything about you."

"Then you would know that I have a big appetite, and since I haven't eaten breakfast this morning, I'm starved."

"Really. Food, yeah I never thought of that but then I didn't think…" He set the fire up then turned to me: "I'll just go get some food. I shan't be long." With that he was gone.

Frantically, I set about trying to break through the tape. I got through the first layer and my hands slip and I cut my wrist on the nail. Wincing, I continue to break through the next layer and eventually my hands are free. I bend down and pull the tape from my ankles, and as I free them I have to stifle a scream, as the tape pulls some of my skin off. As I look up, one of the logs fall from the fire on to the floor. I've got to get out of here quick before the whole place goes up. I run for the door and roly-poly out of it, tumbling and falling until eventually, I come to a stop.

I can hear the noise of a car coming towards me as the spirit child appears in front of me.

'Quick, he's coming back. He must have forgotten something.'

He leads me through the forest to a hollow tree. 'Hide here for a while; when he sees the hut's on fire, he will want to get you out.'

As we sit there I ask my spirit friend, 'What happened to you? How did you die?'

'I was taken whilst playing outside my parents' house, then murdered. My body is buried in these woods. Maybe you can help my mother find my body someday.'

'When this is all over bring her to me and lead the way.'

'Sure, she won't rest until she finds me, it was so long ago. She has been unwell for some time but refuses to join me until she has laid my remains to rest. She doesn't understand that what lies underground is just bones, my soul visits her every day.'

'It's hard for people on earth you know, look at the pickle I'm in.'

'I'll check its clear then get you out of here.'

My spirit friend had only been gone for a few moments when he returned to inform me that all is clear. He starts to lead me out from our hiding place and I find myself running after him through some trees. I keep stumbling as the branches around my legs scratch and cut into me. I feel like I've been running for quite some time when one of my sore ankles get caught on something and I tumble forward smacking my face on the ground.

My legs hurt like hell and my head is pounding, yet I know that somehow I need to find the strength to get up and out of here. Someone seems to help me up, but when I look around there is no one there. Where has my spirit friend gone? I think to myself in a complete panic. It's almost dusk and I have no idea where I am. I start to feel deflated as I take a look around me. I have no idea which way to go, when out of the corner of my eye, I see a beautiful wolf and know that it's a sign from spirit that I'm protected from harm.

To my great relief my spirit friend reappears. 'Are you OK?'

'I think so.'

'Can you keep moving? We are nearly out.'

'I hope so.' We progress on through the trees and suddenly I can hear a rumbling noise to the left of me. I stop suddenly, fearful of what it might be, when all of a sudden a load of cattle come charging straight along the path in front of me making me jump. I continue to follow my spirit friend and can hear the sounds of a car in the distance. We are making slow progress towards the noise of what seems to be cars driving on a road.

We have been driving up and down the same road, well more of a dirt track, for the past half hour and I'm starting to wonder if Rose really knows what she's doing. *Are we ever going to find her?* I wonder.

"Slow down, Chris, she's here, I can feel it. Why haven't we found her? I don't understand it."

As Rose speaks to Chris I look out the window and see someone running out of the woods straight towards the car. Without thinking, I jump out while the car is still moving just as Penny runs into the side of the car. She backward somersaults in the air and somehow I manage to catch her.

"Russell…" she manages to say before she passes out in my arms. Well, it makes a change for her to fall into my arms, I think to myself, and the minute I look down at her I know I'm never letting her go again.

"Call an ambulance." I find myself chocking as I hold her safely in my arms. *Are we too late or is she going to be OK?*

I drop to my knees holding her tightly for fear of losing her again.

Suddenly, there is noise and people all around us and someone keeps shouting in my ears, "Russell, you need to let the paramedics take a look at her."

But I've only just got her back, I think to myself. I can't let her go again. What will they do to her and will she be OK? Oh God, this is just the worst possible feeling in the world.

"Russell, come on, my love, you must let them help her now."

Reluctantly, I pass Penny over to the paramedic as Rose kneels by my side and I sob uncontrollably in her arms.

===== X =====

Chapter Fourteen

I wake suddenly from a deep sleep. *Where am I?* It smells all sterile around me and something has a hold of my hand. I can hear gentle snoring and when I take a look around, I realise I'm lying in a hospital bed with Russell at my side snoring softly. Every bone in my body seems to ache as I raise my hand and gently run my fingers through his hair, tears start to fall down my face as I remember the reason I'm here. How I wish I could stay in this man's arms forever, but it dawns on me with great sadness that this can never be.

"Penny, you're awake. Hey shush, it's alright, baby, I'm never letting you go again."

"But, Russell," I sniff, "what about…"

"Shush, baby, it's OK. We can talk later. Don't upset yourself. I'm here to stay now, everything is going to be alright. That's it, deep breaths, rest easy."

I see Soul out of the corner of my eye: 'Let him take care of you, Penny. I promise this time will be different. When you're ready, you can reveal all to him and he will stay for good, trust me.'

A nurse rushes into the room; she checks all my vitals and informs us that the doctor will be along shortly to talk to us. "You are a very lucky lady. Someone up there must really love you."

Chris comes quietly into the room. "The nurse said you were awake. How are you feeling, Penny? You had us all worried there for a minute."

"Oh, Chris, how long have you been here?"

"Since I got a phone call yesterday from Leigh-Anna asking me to help find you. I've called Brett in to take over from me shortly so that I can go and get some sleep."

"Brett, yes I remember him, he's your best friend from your SAS days."

"That's right, only the best for you will do. Rest assured that Brett and I will be taking it in turns to guard you through this ordeal."

"Leigh-Anna, is she here?"

"I sent her home for some rest, she will be back shortly. Get some rest now. I'll be back soon."

I look to Penny, and although I don't want to leave her, I need to speak to Chris before he goes so I reassure Penny I'll be back in a few minutes and then follow Chris out the door.

"Chris, can I have a quick word before you go."

"Sure, what's up?"

"Do you know what's happening? Did they get the guy that took her?"

"I'm not quite sure at this moment in time. There was talk that, ironically, he may have gone into the hut to rescue her and was killed in the fire. I'll let you know as soon as I can."

"Oh, and, Chris, thanks very much."

"I've known Penny practically all of my life, Russell, so you can rest assure that nothing like this will ever happen again."

"Not if I have anything to do with it," I reply as a rather stocky looking man walks towards us.

Having spent the last forty-eight hours in hospital, it feels really good to be finally going home. It will be so nice to see Barney. Russell said Aunt Megan had brought him and Sky back with her and I'm sure looking forward to seeing them both when I get home. *I've missed that hairy mutt*, I think to myself as Russell helps me into the back of Chris's car. Yeah well, armed escorts from here on in I guess is something I'm going to have to get used to.

I finish running Penny a nice hot bath and go back into the bedroom where I find her staring out of the window, Barney protectively by her side. "Bath's ready, and you shouldn't be out of bed remember, doctor's orders. You were only allowed home if you promised to rest in bed."

"I know, just felt like looking out into the night sky."

"Come, I'll help you in the bath then redress those wounds of yours."

I feel like I've gone ten rounds in a boxing ring as Russell gently helps me into the bath. I lay back in the bubbles and sigh as the warmth soothes me. I don't feel I have the energy to wash myself but at least it is nice to lay back and soak. As if reading my mind, Russell picks up the sponge, smothers it in soap and then gently begins to wash me.

He has been so attentive with me these last few days. After a long soak he helps me out of the bath and gently pats me dry. He dresses my wounds and then he carries me over to the bed where he lays me down and tucks me in, kissing me on the forehead whispering, "Goodnight, beautiful. I love you." *I can't remember ever being this cherished in my life*, I think to myself as I fall asleep.

At some point during the night I must have fallen asleep because I am woken suddenly when Penny begins to fidget next to me. She starts thrashing and fighting with the covers and then she screams and jumps out of the bed. She runs to the corner of the room, so I rush over to her and try to comfort her as loads of people suddenly barge into the room, her eyes look wild as if she's not quite with it. "Get away from me, you are one sick bastard!" she screams as she smacks me around the face. "You will never hurt me again; you sick sorry excuse of a man."

She starts to pound her fists into my ribs as Rose walks into the room. "Penny, it's Rose. I can see him. I'll sort it, calm down."

Penny drops down to the floor and curls into a foetus position, pointing at the corner she yells to Rose, "Get that son of a bitch out of here."

I kneel down and pick her up and carry her over to the bed. I sit on the bed with her on my lap rocking her like a baby. I speak softly to her: "It's OK, baby. No one is ever going to hurt you again. I promise I'll look after you." Finally, I manage to calm her down. I lay her back down in the bed and pull the covers over her, and then gently wash her face with the bowl and sponge that Leigh-Anna had gone downstairs for. "We need to redress your wounds darling," I say softly to her.

"Has he gone, Russell? He was here in this room, over there."

I find myself completely baffled. I didn't see anyone in the room.

"There's no one here, darling. It's alright, you can rest now. I won't let anyone harm you."

"But William, he was here. I see him over there, look in that corner."

I look over to the corner and see nothing. I start to redress her wounds as Rose speaks to her: "Penny, he's gone, my love."

"Did you see him, Rose? What was he doing here? I was being dragged through a forest, and then found myself back in that house trapped with him."

"It's OK, dear, he's gone now."

"Why did he come?"

"He saw what happened to you, and he wanted to make sure you were OK."

"I can't believe after all this time he would just show up; he knows I don't want him anywhere near me. Why would he do that? Why would he frighten me so?"

"I don't think he meant to frighten you; he was concerned for you."

"Concerned, you have to be kidding me right."

"Try to think spiritually, Penny. The ones that hurt us the most stick around the most to make up for the wrongs they done us when they were alive. He has been through his counselling on the other side and is very remorseful for the way he behaved towards you."

"Remorseful, oh please. Did you tell him to stay away?"

"I tried, my dear. I don't think he will be back anytime soon. Try to rest, dear."

"Rose, I am so exhausted." With that Penny closed her

eyes and falls back into a deep sleep.

"Russell, maybe you should go get some ice on that face of yours."

"And leave her, you must be joking, Rose. Rose what did William do to her?"

"Unfortunately, Russell, that is something Penny will have to tell you herself. The only thing I will say was he treated her the worst possible way a man could and unfortunately, he didn't know what he'd had until it was gone. You really should get some ice on that face."

I have been out of hospital for a few days now and the nightmares I've been having are exhausting; they are always the same, bringing back some of the fear that I felt when I was married. I feel like I've lost all the confidence that I'd built back up after my sham of a marriage. Will this ever end? I don't know where I'd be without Russell; he has made me feel so safe, and it sure is comforting, although a little tiring sometimes having everyone here with me.

===== X =====

Chapter Fifteen

I make my way down the garden to the meditation room with Rose, Barney leading the way, like the loyal protector that he is. These last few days have been exhausting. The nightmares are never ending and poor Russell is black and blue from me lashing out at him. He has been so sweet and understanding bless him, I only hope this healing session with Rose helps to elevate these nightmares. God only knows what I'll do to him in my sleep state otherwise. I did suggest he sleeps in one of the other bedrooms but he won't hear of it…come to think of it, he hasn't left my side since he found me, which makes me wonder how Rose managed to persuade him to let me walk down to the meditation room without him.

Leigh-Anna is standing guard on the door as we make our way into the meditation room ready for one of Rose's magical healing sessions. I can feel the warmth of the fire Rose has burning in the fireplace. The room smells of that soothing incense I like and I can feel the comforting, calming presence of spirit all around me. As exhausted as my body feels from the kidnap and nightmares, I'm glad Rose suggested coming down here. I lay on the healing bed, feeling completely calm and relaxed, I gently close my eyes as I prepare to accept the healing Rose and the angels bring to this tired battered body of mine.

"You realise that spirit will have you working overtime once you're fully recovered."

"Of course, Rose. I wouldn't expect it any other way."

"Now, let's get you sorted, ready."

"Um, as I'll ever be."

"Good, let the healing begin."

In the distance I hear Rose asking the healing angels to use her as a channel for the healing energy. After all, that's what we healers are, a channel the angels use to bring healing through our hands or spoken words to soothe a person's physical being, bringing it in line with the inner soul. It has been said that healing begins within, where the answers to our questions lie.

As Rose places her hands over my body, I can feel the heat and tingling energy moving through me, comforting and healing where the angels know it's needed the most. I find myself floating as the spiritual energies flow around me in different colour forms. I see beautiful smoke like colours of blue, pink, greens and yellows as Rose changes her positions. I could lie here all day, but all too soon I feel myself floating back down to earth as Rose gently finishes the healing given thanks – as we always do – to the angels for using her as a channel for the beautiful healing energy we have exchanged during the session.

"How are you feeling, Penny?"

"Relaxed, very relaxed."

"That was a good healing session. I was wondering if you felt strong enough to try connecting to William's energy."

"Rose, I can't believe you're even suggesting…"

"I know, I know, but hear me out."

"Go on."

"I've been thinking; the dreams they are all the same. You being taken, but not by the man who kidnapped you, always by William."

"Yes, so what are you trying to say?"

"William, well yes, he was a complete and utter arse, but you have to agree you've blocked him from any kind of contact with you."

"Well yes, you can't blame me for that."

"No, I understand you completely, it's just that, what I'm trying to say, is if you let him apologise, then you might be able to find some kind of closure. The kidnapping has obviously brought up some deep routed inner issues that maybe you thought you'd dealt with and haven't. So facing him, hearing him out as he is now might help with that."

"I understand what you're saying, it's just that I don't know. He done so much damage."

"As a soul now he realises what he did was wrong. You know what they say, the ones that hurt us the most, stick around the most to make up for all the wrongs. So, maybe if you heard him out with me here, the nightmares would stop. He can do you no harm now."

"What do you suggest?" I can feel the presence of a spirit within the room, which causes the hairs on the back of my neck to stand up. "He's here, isn't he? I can feel his presence, Rose."

"Don't get yourself in a panic; feel the fear then face it head on, no harm is going to come to you."

"Right, let's do this then."

I take a deep breath and then prepare to have one of the most difficult conversations of my life.

'What do you want from me?' I find myself asking William within my own mind.

'Forgiveness.'

'I've forgiven, forgotten and moved on, which means I don't have to let you back into my life.'

'I know, what I did to you was so wrong and I can't apologise enough. Russell...'

'Don't you dare bring him into this...'

'Hear me out please.'

'Well, you have my attention now. Have you been entering my dreams?'

'Not in the bad way you are thinking?'

'Well, they sure as hell don't feel good to me.'

'It's your inner fear, from being taken and feeling trapped when you were with me.'

'Go on.'

'Well, you may have moved on in a sense but Russell, he wants to spend his life with you. Your experience of marriage with me scarred you so bad. He's such a good man, the kind of man I should have been, but wasn't. Our time together was really bad, I understand that now. I was wrong to treat you the way I did, but don't live your life in fear of marriage because of what I did to you. You are only punishing yourself if you spend the rest of your life alone.'

'I don't know what to say to you in answer to that.'

'No two people are the same. I wish I had known then what I know now, I'd have lived my life differently and shown you the respect you deserve.'

'It's a little late for all that now.'

'Never too late for anything. I'm so sorry for all the wrongs I done you. I will always be there for you if you ever need my help just ask. Thank you for listening, I will always love you, you know.' And with that he was gone.

"Thank you for the healing, Rose. I think I need to go and lie down now."

"When we get to the house, maybe it is time for you to open up to Russell...tell him the story about William and you. I know it is difficult for you to relive those times but it might help with the healing process."

"I'm not sure I'm ready. How is he going to feel having used goods and the fact I can't give him a child?"

"Don't ever let me here you say that about yourself again. That man loves you for you, and he doesn't care about anything else. You should have seen him when we found you and he thought we were too late...cried in my arms like a baby he did. And get over that independent streak, young lady, and let your forever after man look after you from now on."

"I have been letting him take care of me."

"I'm on about forever."

I have been pacing up and down for the past half-hour or more. How long are they going to be? Maybe I should go and check and make sure they are OK. No, I promised Rose I'd leave her to it. I stop to look out of the French doors down the garden and feel relieved to see them making their way back up the garden towards the house. That's when my stomach churned. I could see Barney's ears prick up and he ferociously dashes down the garden towards the hedge, closely followed by Leigh-Anna.

"Chris, Brett!" I bellow as I fling open the French doors and run down the garden towards Penny and Rose.

Chris runs straight past me closely followed by Brett. "Russell, get Penny in the house, take this." He flings a gun towards me as he runs past.

I lead Penny and Rose back to the house and wait with them for the others to return.

After what seems like an age, Leigh-Anna returns to us with Barney who protectively takes to Penny's side. Absentmindedly, she pets him while looking lost in thought. Eventually, she speaks: "The stalker, he didn't die in the fire at the hut, he's still out there isn't he."

"Robert, that's his first name, completely obsessed with you," Rose pipes in.

"Rose, I'm not sure you're helping, but thanks for the name. I'll let Chris know. Penny, we only found out late last night. There is no evidence at the burnt down hut of any human remains, and unfortunately, because of the fire, there is little DNA to go on."

"Right, that's it, Penny. I'm getting you out of here. Go pack a case."

"But, Russell, I can't just leave."

"You can and we will. As soon as Chris and Brett get back, we are going to Italy. My father's friend owns a hotel out there where we can stay and I know that you will be safe."

"What about Barney and everything here? We can't just up and leave."

"Your aunt can take care of Barney and Rose can continue to sort things out here. It's only until you're feeling stronger. Chris and Leigh-Anna can come with us, just to be on the safe side, and Brett can look after Rose and your aunt."

"I'll help you pack," Rose offers.

I feel too tired to argue, so I nod slowly then make my way towards the door, Rose following behind me. "Penny," Rose sighs. "While you're away, do me a favour and tell that man in there your story."

"I'll try, Rose, I'll try."

===== X =====

Chapter Sixteen

After one of the most interesting flights I've ever been on, what with an abandoned first take-off then more turbulence and plane bouncing than I'd ever experienced before, we finally land at Naples Airport. We retrieve our bags and after a tedious hour-long coach journey, we arrive at a beautiful hotel in Sorrento. Our room overlooks the sea and as I look out of the balcony, I take in a long cleansing breath and think to myself that this is just what I need to recover. Sun, sand, sea and plenty of rest.

"How's the view, darling?"

"Beautiful, this is just what I needed, thank you."

"You don't need to thank me. Chris and Leigh-Anna have the room next door. They are waiting outside to take us down to dinner, but if you're not up to it, I'll let them know we're having room service."

"No that's fine, we'll go down to dinner."

The dining room was out of this world. There was a buffet with various different choices of pastas and salads fancily laid out for the guests to help themselves. I chose some kind of pasta dish that was full of chicken topped with a white sauce and it tasted delicious. After a few glasses of wine, I was starting to feel a lot more relaxed than I'd felt back home. In the corner of the restaurant was a grand piano, it was truly beautiful. Russell excused himself from the table and, much to my surprise, went over to the grand piano.

He lifted the lid and began to play what sounded like the tune for the prayer Ava Maria, it was absolutely beautiful, and everybody applauded once he'd finished. One of the waitresses said something to him and he nodded: "For you, Penny, my love." And he played again as the waitress sang in Italian what sounded like a love song, but not knowing Italian myself, I wasn't quite sure, but either way it sounded beautiful.

"I never knew you played the piano."

"I love to play, even wanted to be a pianist at one stage but life got in the way."

"What was the song about?"

"A beautiful lady, fitting for you I thought."

When we arrived back in our room we sat on the balcony with a glass of wine staring out into the beautiful evening sunset. Suddenly, Russell bent down on one knee and said, "Penny, this whole kidnapping business, it really scared the shit out of me. I can't live without you in my life, so please be my wife, to have and to hold forever."

That's when I knew I had to somehow reveal my story to him, so that he understood my fears of marriage.

"Russell, there are some things you should know about my past before..."

"This is about William isn't it?" he said as he stood.

"Well, you need to know, as it might change your opinion about marriage."

"Nothing you can say will change my mind about marrying you, but if it helps, then I will sit and listen."

He takes his seat once again and looks across at me. I down the remainder of my glass of wine and then prepare to reveal my story to him.

"When I was born, I was born into this world with nothing; my mother died in child birth, and that's why I was brought up by my Aunt Megan. Ever since I can remember I've had this spiritual gift that I guess at some points during my younger years made me seem different to others. I always felt different from other children. People would say I was a loner because I used to play on my own and talk to myself a lot. The thing is people didn't see what I saw. I was never alone as I was always talking to my spiritual friends.

"When I was old enough to understand, my aunt decided to tell me about my mother. She sat me down one day with this photo album and I looked at her and said, 'I already know.' She looked at me with tears in her eyes when I described my mother without even looking at the pictures. I told her that she regularly played with me when I played with my dolls. I remember my aunt saying, 'Penny, you have been blessed with my grandmother's most amazing gift.' I felt really special that day.

"Anyhow, as I started school, I didn't have any friends and would stay in the corner of the playground watching others play. It used to baffle me why they were so horrible to each other; my spirit friends weren't at all like that, and they always played with me lovingly. About three months into school, Leigh-Anna started. Being the new girl in the playground, she was pretty much like me, kept herself to herself. So one day, I started talking to her and from that day on we became the best of friends.

"As I grew older my spiritual gifts seem to get put on hold so to speak. I had a new friend to play and explore with, and boy did we explore; we were little devils sometimes. I remember playing in the paddling pool and this one time we dunked the cat in it with us. The poor thing looked just like a drowned rat. We started high school together and became the terrible twosome; we both hated school and would bunk off at every occasion. Neither one of us was very academically clever; maths was our worst subject…we hardly went to the lesson. We got caught in the end you know, and ended up on report. Those were the days. We were terrors, but we sure lived a lot.

"It all changed a bit when I was fourteen years old and my uncle died. I was close to him you see and missed him terribly. Leigh-Anna and I would go to the park and get completely drunk on some bottle or other that we'd nicked out of Megan's cupboard. I started dating a boy from school around the same time I got my first little Saturday job. There was this one time we met him at the park and I stupidly got so drunk that I ended up sleeping with him.

"The next day the whole school knew and I became the easy lay. Annoying really, a man could have a hundred girls and he'd be a stud, whereas a girl does it once and she's a slag. Needless to say we broke up and my school life just got worse, that was until I was fifteen and met Zac. My aunt didn't approve of him as he was nineteen, so she tried to stop me seeing him and I was quite the bitch, I'd leave her horrible notes saying I hated her. She'd try to tell me that he was using me but I just wouldn't listen, that was until I saw him with this other girl. So you see, there are a lot of things I said and done when I was younger that I'm not proud of, but I guess I was a young girl maturing and experimenting with life. I like to think it shaped me into being the good person that I am today.

"Then there was William. I met him when I was seventeen years old...too young really. To start with I thought the world of him, and he could do no wrong in my eyes. We got married when I was twenty and I remember having a few doubts even then. The night before we married, Leigh-Anna said to me, 'Penny, you don't have to do this you know.' I think she knew that deep down he wasn't the right man for me. Being a spiritual person doesn't somehow make you able to look at your own life and know how things are going to turn out. Funny isn't it, I can see so many things for others, help so many other people, but when it comes to my own life I go blank. Maybe I didn't want to see, I don't know.

"Anyhow, he had me fooled that's for sure; he seemed reliable at the time and behind all his strange little ways – we all have strange ways – I could only see a good man. Looking back now, I couldn't have been more wrong. It started with small things really like if I wore my hair up he'd pull it out and say you don't want to look like Dumbo with those ears of yours sticking out. I guess I just thought that's the way men are, that's the way they treat their ladies and I guess it become the norm. But what I started to realise as time went on was that I deserved to be treated with more respect and to be accepted for being the way I was.

"When we used to go out, even before we got married, he used to be so judgemental. I mean in the sense that if I didn't wear things that he wanted me to wear he would make comments like, 'You're not wearing that are you' or 'Oh, no, you're not wearing those shoes are you.' I'd spend hours and hours getting ready sometimes and my efforts never quite felt good enough. His idea of a compliment was, 'You look doable tonight.'

"That was only if he noticed and liked the effort that I'd made. On those occasions, in fact on every occasion, it was as if I had to meet with his approval. The doable thing I guess would have been OK if it had made me feel like he actually meant it, but he would spend the evening eyeballing all the other women that were at the same club, restaurant, bar or where ever we went. He would often make comments like, 'Why don't you wear things like that?' It was like he wanted a trophy on his arm to show off, which I guess all men want to show off their women, but surely by making them feel good about themselves.

"Sometimes I would feel so hurt that I would bring it up when we got home, but he would twist things and say, 'I'm sure you imagine half these things, I never said that.' I used to question myself a lot, thinking that maybe I'd misunderstood what he'd said, but there was always this little voice in my head that said, 'I know what I heard.' I guess it just became the norm. Strange, thinking about it now, but it actually felt normal at the time.

"I started to doubt my own abilities as a woman, and I never quite felt good enough. My confidence, self-esteem and self-worth took quite a nosedive and I became self-conscious about my appearance to the point that I would ask for his approval about the things that I was wearing. Can you believe that? Me asking for someone's approval, really how absurd? I started to wonder at this stage if this was really love; surely if someone loves you, they accept you for what you are and how you look, not for what you can and could be. Still, I married him anyway. You see at the time, I thought the world of him. I really loved him.

"Stupid uh. Anyway, I gave my job up for him because it was what he wanted me to do. I travelled around with him to different locations while he rode his bike at different races and supported him along the way. That's when things first began to change. I wasn't working so I couldn't pay for the things I wanted. My independence had gone along with my freedom. He made me sell my car saying that I couldn't keep it on the road with no pay check and to top it all I was away from Leigh-Anna and my Aunt Megan. He kept saying that if I wanted things I'd have to work for them, but I couldn't do that while I was at his side supporting him. He could have anything he wanted and he did have everything he wanted and that's when the resentment set in, which is not good in any marriage. I was starting to feel that our relationship was based on control, him trying to control me, which is most definitely not love. The more he tried to control me, the more resentful I became."

I am lost in my own thoughts for a while as the darkness surrounds me ones again, knowing that somehow I'd got to tell Russell the full truth as best I could.

"Go on, Penny, I promise to listen without judgement."

"You sure you want to hear this without walking away from used goods?"

"Used goods! Don't ever say that about yourself again. I love you, be assured whatever happened is in the past and I will never ever walk away from you."

I take a deep breath and then continue: "God, I'd even dress up for him in the bedroom just to make him happy, because it was what he wanted. Yeah, I guess it's every man's fantasy, to see his woman wearing a police outfit or a nurse's outfit and so forth. I hated it all, but anything to keep the peace. The sex was always a disappointment. I'd get him all excited you know by sucking him off, but when it came to me, his way of exciting me was to wet his finger with his spit then rub it against my folds before he'd pound into me. It was so unsexy and more often than not, uncomfortable.

"He'd always come before I was ready, and then when

he was done, he'd simply roll over and fall asleep. There was no cuddling or 'I love you', just satisfaction for him and disappointment for me. It was like 'wham, bam, thank you mam'.

"Then things got worse, a lot worse. I couldn't fall pregnant, give him the child he needed to carry on the family name. I suddenly became useless or at least that's what he used to say to me and how he used to make me feel. I started to paint when we were home to help relieve the pressure I felt, but he was never encouraging. He just used to make comments like, 'That's awful. What you doing you weirdo?' or 'Why do you want to do that? When I give you everything!' But the truth be told he only thought about himself. That's why I started to sell my art at markets so that I could get some pocket money. It was hard getting motivated when someone knocked you at every turn, but I found the strength from somewhere.

"I wanted to put a small art studio in the garden for my artwork, but his answer to this was, 'It will be a waste of time; why do you want to paint anyway?' He didn't understand my need for some independence. So, without his help, I started dismantling the rockery at the end of the garden, which meant lugging heavy loads of soil in the wheelbarrow. All the time he watched me and made snide comments like, 'What are you doing?' and 'You're making a right mess in this garden.' There was no support from him. God, I even laid the slabs for the studio. I sold a good few paintings and made enough for a small studio and, when it came, he finally agreed under protest to help put it together, much to my surprise.

"When people came round he would say things like, 'Look at what I done for her' and take all the credit for my hard work. Other people would complement my art work but to my face he would make remarks like, 'That doesn't look right,' but to others he would say how wonderful my work was, it was a complete contradiction. As if all this wasn't bad enough, he started drinking, really heavily. He'd go out really early and come home really late smelling of women's perfume. If I said anything he would grab me by the arms, leaving bruises and say, 'Live with it, bitch.' He was a different man when he drank and scared the living daylights out of me.

"Gradually, things got really bad. He came home one night really drunk and hit me so hard that I passed out, and when I woke I couldn't open my eye. He was snoring loudly on the bed. He'd fucked me whilst I was laying out cold on the floor and then gone to sleep in the nice comfy bed, leaving me on the floor. So I guess if your husband can rape you, that's how it felt that night. His mother came round a few days afterwards; seeing the bruises her only comments were, 'What do you expect when you can't give him what he needs,' and that I couldn't keep a man happy if I tried.

"So, I became his living punch bag; he took all his anger and frustration out on me, often leaving me black and blue. I would be so sore sometimes by the aggressive way he fucked me, and there were times when I thought he would rip me in two. I was really scared of him and didn't know who to turn to.

"Sometimes he would apologise the next day and say how he'd never hit me again. This one time I said I was leaving if he didn't stop drinking; boy, was that the wrong thing to say. He fucked and beat me really bad that day, while telling me that no one else would want me, that I was fat and ugly. Then, not long after that, this one time he came home…it was really bad. I could see it in his eyes, I don't quite know…"

"I'm listening, Penny, it's OK, honey, no one will ever hurt you again, I promise."

"He charged towards me and pushed my face down on the bed, and then he pulled my hand above my head and tied them to the top of the bed frame. I was screaming and crying so he grabbed me around the throat and squeezed me around the neck shouting: 'Shut up, you whore! I know you love it when I push my cock into you. Well, guess what, I've got a nice surprise for you tonight, something different, you're going to love it.' I screamed and begged him to untie my hands but he ignored me while he removed my underwear, then once again he wrapped his hands around my throat and forced his cock into my arse. In all my life I'd never felt pain like it. I thought I was going to die. The more I screamed, the more he loved it. Finally, when he'd finished with me he untied me and said, 'Get dressed, you lazy bitch.'

"That night was the turning point; as soon as he fell asleep, I ran for my life. To start with I didn't know where to go, I was bleeding really badly. That's when I bumped into Rose, who changed my life forever that night. She took me to a safe house, stayed with me, cared for me. It took me ages and I mean ages to heal from the things that William had done to me. The physical scars healed quite quickly but the mental scars, I think will stay with me a lifetime. Rose helped me to bring back out my spiritual gift and I realised that I needed to experience the things I did in order to be able to help others and give them the understanding they needed.

"The next thing I heard of William was that he'd been killed in a motorbike race somewhere in Brazil. Can you believe that, I actually felt guilty for feeling relieved. The house went to his mother and I started to rebuild my life as a free independent woman. I swore then that I'd never re-marry and put myself in that vulnerable position again. I'd never let another man control anything in my life again. Even now I sometimes feel like used goods not worthy of being loved. Can you understand my reasons now?"

For a long time, Russell sat staring at me and I was starting to think that maybe he wanted out. There was still that part of me that felt insecure from my experience, that voice that said it was my fault, as if I had allowed it all to happen. I looked at Russell and I had no idea what he was thinking. However, he stood up and came over to me, pressing his forehead to mine, he said, "You are so beautiful; no person should have to go through those things. It's just as well he's dead because right now, I would probably kill him myself." He lifted me into his arms and walked over to the bed and then gently lay me down. Pulling the cover over me, he climbed in next to me and wrapped his arms around me. Kissing me on the forehead he said, "Sleep now, my beautiful angel. I'll be here when you wake in the morning."

"One thing I realised, Russell, is that it's not just women that suffer this kind of abuse. Men do too. It's just as awful for them you know. Most of the time they find it hard to ask for help because they are a man being abused by a woman."

I yawn rather loudly then fall into a blissful sleep wrapped in the arms of the most remarkable man I've ever met. Comforted by the knowledge that despite him knowing all of my truths, he would still be there in the morning when I woke up.

===== X =====

Chapter Seventeen

As I stir awake it feels like someone's eyes are on me. I feel hot and bothered as the sun's rays fill the bedroom. "Morning, my beautiful lady, did I ever tell you that even in sleep you are the most beautiful person I've ever met."

"Morning, handsome," I respond as I yawn and stretch. I start to clamber out of bed so that I can use the bathroom, but I'm overcome by a dizzy feeling and almost fall back on to the bed.

"Careful, gorgeous lady of mine," Russell says as his strong arms catch me. "Let me help you…can't have you falling over now can I."

"Are you going to watch me pee?"

"Even when you're peeing you look beautiful."

"Get out of here you big oaf," I say throwing the toilet roll at him.

I can hear him chuckling away to himself as I finish with business then start the shower. I start to climb in when dizziness falls over me once again and a slight squeal escapes my lips as I begin to slip. Two strong arms catch me as I fall. "Thanks, I must have drunk too much wine last night."

"Come, let's shower together. I want to kiss every part of that beautiful body of yours."

Gently Russell helps me into the shower and climbs in behind me. I hate feeling so weak; my body still aches everywhere and I feel so weary. He picks up the sponge and soaps it up and begins to carefully wash me. Once he's happy he turns me around to face him and gently kisses me on the lips. "Have I ever told you your lips are beautiful." Cupping my cheeks in both hands he kisses me gently. "Those eyes and cheeks of yours are sensational."

He kisses each part of my body, and when he's finished he lifts me from the shower and gently pats me dry before wrapping a bath robe around me and carrying me back over to the bed where he lays me down before going to

112

finish his own shower.

When he emerges from the shower with a small towel wrapped around his waist I can't take my eyes off his muscular body. "If I didn't feel so damned weak I'd throw you on this bed." He kisses me gently on the cheek. "We have a lifetime of exploring together, my beautiful lady. Our needs will keep until you're strong again. I just want you to know that what you told me last night makes no difference whatsoever to me. You experienced some dreadful things that no person should have to experience and I intend to spend the rest of my life making you feel special and showing you just how beautiful any person in their right mind would see you."

"I know you said about marriage last night but what about your family commitments, your parents are expecting grandchildren. Don't get me wrong, you have been so sweet to me looking after me after the kidnapping and everything and I do love you, but are you forgetting why I walked away from you in the first place. I'm not sure I could give you the kind of future you're looking for."

"My family love you, Penny. If it comes to it and if you are ever ready to marry again, then maybe we could adopt. I'm a patient man. One step at a time...marriage when and if you're ever ready."

"What say, for the time being, we exchange promise rings and make a promise to each other to always look after each other, respect each other and be faithful to one another for as long as we both shall live, without the stress of a big white wedding and everything else that goes with it. We could simply go into a jewellery shop while we are here and choose rings, and then exchange them on the beach."

"I like that idea. Did you ever look into why you couldn't fall pregnant?"

"I just never fell, and I guess because my aunt never fell pregnant, I just assumed that I would follow in her footsteps and be childless."

113

"So, if and I mean if you are ever ready to marry and try again, we simply look into it together and if it doesn't work out then I'm happy to remain childless with you. Now let's get breakfast."

After breakfast, which consisted of croissants and coffee, I began to feel better so suggested grabbing a lounger by the pool. Occasionally, I glance over at Russell and each time I glance at him he's looking directly at me. I can't help thinking to myself that I've never been around a man who only seems to have eyes for me before, and as if reading my expression Russell says, "I only have eyes for you, my love. The most beautiful lady in the whole wide world."

"You should be careful with the mind reading you know; if spirit catches on, they'll have you working away." I laugh.

"There's only one person's mind I wish to read and she's staring right at me." Leaning over he kisses me sweetly on the lips.

After spending three days sat around the pool relaxing and being thoroughly pampered, my body finally starts to feel stronger. So, on arriving back from dinner, I push Russell down on to the bed and start to kiss him passionately. "Are you sure you're OK to do this? I don't want to hurt you."

"I'm more that OK, now get your arse out of those clothes and let me have that cock of yours."

"Yeah, you're definitely feeling better. I can tell you're getting back to normal when your commanding voice starts propositioning me."

I pick up the pillow and start to hit him with it. "You, you're going to pay."

We laugh together as I repeatedly hit him with the pillow. Grabbing the pillow from me he lobs it across the room and turns me around so that I am beneath him. "Now, my beautiful, pretty, sweet, gorgeous lady, I'm going to show you how a real man worships and pleases his lady."

He removes his shirt and then undresses me, kissing my body everywhere as he does so. "Have I told you how much I love this beautiful body of yours?"

"Hum, quite a few times over the last few days."

"Now I'm going to show you."

He grabs my foot and starts to kiss and massage it, and then gradually makes his way towards my most intimate area, kissing and licking up the inside of my leg. "Your legs are so gorgeous, and this between them is a feast fit for a king."

He begins to gently lick and suck at the spot between my legs and I feel an overwhelming sense of pleasure as I lift my hips wildly to meet with his tongue. "Ah, yes!" I scream out as he hits that secret spot inside me that sets me on fire.

"You'll have Chris and Leigh-Anna in here if you keep yelling out."

"Don't care, it feels so good." He continues to caress my body and I run my hands through his hair, tugging it while screaming out with pleasure as he hits that all-important sensitive spot within me and I feel myself coming while screaming out his name. Gently, he pushes his cock into that special place between my legs and I find myself wrapping my legs around him as we find our rhythm together. I feel more alive than I've ever felt before as we move together grunting and groaning while making love. *It's never felt so good,* I think to myself, as I feel him swell inside me. We scream each other's names as we climax together and his semen fills me up inside. Blissfully, we fall asleep together wrapped in each other's arms.

I hear the shower running as the sun's rays fill the hotel room, and stretching, I roll out of bed and make my way into the bathroom where the sight of Russell's body behind the curtain has me turned on. I step into the shower with him, pushing him up against the wall I kiss him passionately before going down on to my knees and taking his cock into my mouth. Wildly, I suck on his cock and caress his balls "Ah," he screams with pleasure as I tease his cock with my mouth. I rise and wrap my legs around his waist and lower myself on to his cock and ride him wildly. We scream out together as we find our release.

"Wow, what a greeting. Good morning, beautiful, fancy some sightseeing today then a look in the jewellers for that promise ring," Russell manages to speak once he gets his breath back.

"Sounds like a good idea."

"Great, let's go get breakfast and then get going."

Chris drives us along the winding roads towards the village of Pompeii and as the car approaches, I feel the coldness and airy silence of the village, which at one time must have been a thriving beautiful place. Russell holds on to my hand and we begin to walk around the ruins. I can sense the panic of the village people all around me when the volcano irrupted and coated this quiet place with lava.

We walk past rubble and crumbled buildings and come across the body of a child, which is preserved in what looks like cement and in front of the child lies a pregnant mother. The place holds a chilling silence as I close my eyes and visualise what the village used to be. In my mind's eye, I can see friendly happy people surrounded by beautiful homes and flowers. Then my vision changes and I become chilled right through to the bone as I see the terror in people's faces. I hear the ground rumble and see people running and screaming for their lives as they try to avoid being coated in thick hot lava. I see the child and mother before me crying out in pain as the lava from the volcano coats their bodies.

As we walk further through this fallen village, I come across a spirit child looking lost and confused and know that I was meant to come here today to help this poor lost soul. In my own mind I speak to the child in front of me: 'Hello, my name's Penny. Are you lost?' The child talks to me in Italian but strangely enough I understand what he is saying. He has been looking for his Mum but can't find her. He asks me how come I can hear him as people come and go but just ignore him. He tells me that his name is Dino and that some of the children from the village come and play with him sometimes. 'They keep telling me to go through this tunnel to the light, but I am afraid to go without my mother.'

'Have they told you about what's within the light? Maybe your mother awaits you there. What was her name?'

'Enzo, that's my friend, he says that it is peaceful there with lots of beautiful people. My mother was called Claudia and my father Franco. Who is that funny man standing next to you? He is just like the children, he appeared from out of nowhere. They do that to you know.'

I can hear Soul chuckle in my ear as the boy speaks about him. 'Some people do, his name is Soul and he is a very wise old man. He is what I call my guide and protector; would you like him to help you.'

'I'm not sure, he looks friendly enough. What is that golden light standing next to him? I've seen it before…it comes with the children all of the time.'

'Did you ever go to church with your mother and learn about God and his guardian angels.'

'Sure, we used to go all the time.'

'Then you have nothing to fear…the golden light that you see is the light of Archangel Michael. He is the strong protector of all who live on earth. If there is one being of light that could take you to your mother, it would be Archangel Michael and I think you should trust him.'

Dino walks towards Archangel Michael and I can see him taking the hand that is offered to him. 'Dino, one thing before you go. Give me a sign when you arrive if you find your Mum.'

'What do you mean by a sign?'

'Wave from a cloud in the sky.'

'But how do I do that? There isn't even a cloud in the sky.'

117

'You'll see when you get there. Trust me, it will be wonderful.'

'OK. I'll try. Grazie, Bella Signora.'

I continue to walk through the village following Russell and as we prepare to leave, I feel the urge to look up to the sky. I find myself looking into the face of Dino within a single cloud that has formed and as I acknowledge his presence he smiles and waves at me. What a wonderful world this is and I wish him God bless and thank Archangel Michael for helping him.

When we return to the village of Sorrento, Chris drives us through the town where we find this small jewellery shop. We pick out two heart-shaped signet rings with a diamond in the centre, and whilst we wait for our initials to be imprinted into them, we look around at the various different pieces of jewellery that are on display. Having paid for the rings we make our way to the beach and once we settle into a nice spot, Russell gets down on one knee and slides the ring on to my finger saying, "Penny, please accept this ring as a sign of my promise to be faithful, love and cherish you with all of my heart for as long as we both shall live."

"I accept. Russell. I give you this ring as a token of my promise to you. I promise to love, be faithful and cherish you for as long as we both shall live."

As we seal the promise with a kiss I can hear Chris and Leigh-Anna cheering.

We sit on the beach and watch as the sun sets over the beautiful sea, and Russell asks me why I was so vacant looking, whilst we were at Pompeii. I find myself telling him all about little Dino and how I reassured him so that he could meet with his parents in the afterlife.

"So, do you see spirits everywhere? Like when you walk down the street, do you constantly see them and know everything about them?"

Smiling, I answer him as best I can: "It's a little hard to explain it all but I will do my best. Sometimes I see people out of the blue when they need urgent help, but having

118

said that it's not with me all of the time. I kind of switch the button on and off if you like, and most of the time I raise my vibration to meet there's. How can I explain this now…? Remember, I told you it's like living two lives."

"Yes, I remember, you told me a while ago."

"That's right, well everybody in this life and in the next life live on a kind of energy vibration. Earth evolves at a lower vibration to that of which we know as heaven does. So, I kind of suppose while souls bring their energy vibration down to our level, we raise ours to meet them halfway. If you can imagine fine tuning a radio to get the right frequency, then I guess that would be the correct way to describe it. It takes a lot of effort and energy on both parts and can be exhausting to start with but of course, like with most things, the more you do it the easier it becomes. There are different ways in which spirits communicates with us."

"In which way?"

"Well, there is that little idea within your own mind that keeps popping up all the time, and try as much as you like to brush it to one side, it keeps popping into your head. This is one way that they communicate to us, giving us ideas and supporting us when we need them there."

"So how does an actual medium like yourself work?"

"Connection comes in different ways; we call it clairsentience, clairaudience, clairvoyance."

"What does all that mean?"

"Before I go on stage, I open my energy vibration, like fine tuning a radio as I explained earlier. In this state I am open to the energies around me and become what we would call clairsentience, meaning sensitive to spiritual energies. This is how most mediums work. You begin to know things about people without seeing proof, as spirits put ideas into you head and communicate information that way. It's a knowing without actually seeing and requires a great deal of trust. I pick up on the energies by feelings. I can feel cold breezes as spirits get close to me. Sometimes I feel them touch me and get tingling sensations. If a spirit died of a heart attack for example, I may feel a pain within my chest.

"Imagine fine tuning that radio station and you can hear a buzzing within your ears as you find the right frequency or radio station that you are looking for. Well, in spiritual terms, this is clairaudience and as I raise my vibration I can tune into spirits and hear the voices of them when they connect and tell me what message they wish me to pass on to a loved one. Clairvoyance doesn't happen all of the time, but this simply means clearly seeing spirits and once I'm tuned into the zone as I call it sometimes, spirits choose to show themselves to me as they were in the human body. Remember, when you die you become an energy form again, kind of like an orb, a spinning ball of light, and it takes a lot of effort on their behalf to show themselves in this way and I am always honoured when they do. When open to spirit communication, I can also see things play out in what spiritual people call my third eye. By expanding and being open to receiving information, events can unfold within your mind through your third eye."

"The sunset looks beautiful here."

"Just like you, my love. Your spiritual work is fascinating."

"You know we should be heading home; there's a show I need to do in a few days."

"I'd never stop you doing anything and I fully support all that you do. But according to Chris the stalker is still out there and I worry for your safety."

"I know you do, but we have to return sooner or later. I feel stronger now and we can't stay away forever. We both have commitments. Thank you for looking after me so well."

"It was my pleasure, you know I promise to look after you forever, Penny, you're the only one for me."

"You are so sweet, Russell, I only wish that I had met you sooner."

"I love you, my beautiful lady, and when you're a hundred years old, you will still be beautiful in my eyes."

"I love you too, Russell."

"Promise me one thing more; when we get home, you won't go anywhere alone. It's just until this stalker is caught."

"Like Chris or Leigh-Anna are going to let me out of there sight, I mean look at them, constantly on the alert. I couldn't get away if I tried."

"Please, promise me."

"If it makes you feel better, I promise."

The next day we board a flight home feeling relaxed and refreshed from our escape in the sun.

Chapter Eighteen

I sit at my vanity desk looking at my reflection in the mirror, and although I'm almost back to my normal strong self, I can't help feeling slightly nervous going back on stage knowing that my stalker is still out there somewhere. As I view my reflection, I notice that I'm looking a bit paler than normal and come to think of it, I have been feeling rather sick in the stomach since I've been back. Probably the change in water from the holiday, I think to myself as I prepare myself to face the audience outside my dressing room. Soul my beautiful guide, appears behind me speaking within my mind: 'Penny, dear, I just wanted to let you know. You are completely safe tonight; we do have an important job for you to do later…all will be revealed and when this show is over, you need to get yourself a pregnancy test.'

What? I think to myself. *That's just not possible.* 'I see all your thoughts don't forget, it is possible, the problem wasn't so much you couldn't have children. More the fact you couldn't relax enough with William and, in case you have forgotten, you weren't exactly careful while you were away.' I make my way to the stage, and can't believe that this can be true. *I can't be. Could I?*

'Have you been watching me?' I joke with my spirit guide.

'Now you know we would never interfere in your privacy.'

'I know, I know,' I say as I make my way on to the stage to greet the audience in front of me.

I give my usual welcome and explanation of my work, and as I look up to find that all important light, I catch the eye of someone that looks like the man who took me. My legs turn to jelly and I pause with a sense of unease, when suddenly I feel Soul's strong presence behind me. 'Penny that's not him. You are completely safe. We need you to do important work tonight when this show is over. I give you all of my strength and power. Do you want me to take over?'

'I'm sorry, Soul, but I think I may well need you to.'

Suddenly I feel Soul enter me from behind and I feel him take control of my body.

"Rose what just happened? Penny she looks different."

"I think I'm needed on stage; don't worry, she will be fine. It's called trance work."

The audience are very quiet as I step onto stage with a chair.

"Penny dear, would you like to sit down?" Penny slowly nods her head and I help her into the chair. Turning, I face the audience and tell them who I am and explain what has happened the best way I can.

While Soul takes over Penny's body, I give a reassuring explanation to the audience and then continue where Penny left off and begin to give a message to a young gentleman in the front row. Suddenly, Penny stands tall and strong, and then between us, we continue to work through some of the people in the audience. This is certainly different, I think to myself as we end the first half of the show with wise words from Soul.

'The world would be a much better place if everyone learnt how to live their lives in peace instead of trying to outdo one another – work together. See yourself and everyone around you through eyes only of love and not hatred. Live in harmony together, and except each other for who you are. This is what the angels and your guides want for you – love and peace.'

I help Penny off stage, sit her down and allow her some time to sit quiet as Soul leaves her body and she changes back to her usual self. "What happened back there?"

"Thank you for helping, Rose. I lost it for a minute. I thought the stalker was out there. I just couldn't focus so Soul took over."

"Don't tell Russell that. Maybe it was too soon to go back on stage."

"No, I'll be fine, I'm needed tonight. I'll be fine the second half...just give me a minute."

"OK, if you're sure."

Rose accompanies me back on stage for the second half of the show, along with Soul of course, and that's when I realise what I'm supposed to do this evening. There to greet me in the centre of the stage is my little spirit child, the one that helped me escape from the crazy stalker.

He really is one of the most beautiful looking children I have ever seen. I never really noticed it before, but I guess you don't when you're trying to escape from a mad man. He has beautiful blonde wavy hair and light blue eyes that smile at you. They say that the eyes are the route to the soul and I can tell that this little boy certainly does have a beautiful soul, which makes it all the more difficult to wonder how someone could cut his life so short. I nod to him in acknowledgement and in my own mind ask him to take me to his mother, while turning to face the audience I use my usual welcome back. I look up to find his beautiful light shining and hovering above the audience.

I follow his glow to a frail elderly lady in the front row and notice the familiarity. He certainly took after his mother in the looks department, whose blue eyes staring up at me are the same as the spirit child who helped me escape a few weeks ago. I can only imagine how beautiful she would have looked in her younger days, but as I ask Eugene to move the camera to the front row, I notice that her energy field is dull and there is a certain weakness surrounding her. I know that her time in this world is limited, so time is not on our side.

"Margaret, my dear, I can see you are frail, so I won't ask you to stand but can you please confirm to me that you have a child in spirit. A child that was taken from this world in tragic circumstances."

She nods at me through tearful eyes.

"I would like to let you know that Zac is standing right behind you, with his hand on your shoulder. He says to tell you that he is well and enjoying his new life. He doesn't want you to worry about him anymore; in fact, he is awaiting your arrival. He says that you have been looking for his resting place for a long time now, and although it doesn't matter to him that there was no real farewell for him, he also knows that it means a lot to you to lay him to rest before you join him in the next life. Does this all make sense to you?"

"Yes, perfect sense," comes the frail answer.

"I would like to help you. So will send one of my crew over to get you at the end of the show as there is much to discuss privately. This is a very delicate situation, which I feel wouldn't be right to continue in front of such a large audience. How does that sound to you?"

"Can you really help me?"

"Yes, I feel I can."

"I would be most grateful and look forward to seeing you at the end of the show."

"The pleasure would be all mine. I have much to tell you."

Rose and I proceed with the rest of the show, moving around from person to person and passing on different messages, some of which make no sense to me but mean a lot to the recipients. I finish the evening with my usual farewell and make my way off the stage with Rose.

I return to my dressing room where I find Margaret waiting for me. "Margaret, how are you, my dear? Can I get you anything to drink?" I ask as I take some water out of the refrigerator.

"Not for me thank you."

I take a seat next to Margaret and grab hold of her frail hand as I prepare to tell her about my meeting with her son.

"Your son is a very special soul. Very few people know this, but a few weeks ago I was taken by a crazy stalker whilst out walking through some woods in the New Forest.

I don't quite remember what happened; one minute I was walking through the trees listening to the birds singing and the next minute, I woke in some kind of make-shift hut tied to a chair. When I looked around at my surroundings, your son's spirit was there. At the time I didn't realise what a handsome little boy he was. But when I walked on that stage tonight for the second half of the evening, I saw him properly for the first time. He has your eyes."

"He did have my eyes. When he was a baby, people would say to me, what a beautiful baby he was."

"Well as you can imagine at the time, I was in rather a difficult position. Tied to a chair and not really knowing who had taken me and how I was going to get out of the hut. Well, that day your son was my hero. He guided me out of that hut and back through the trees to a road where I was saved from whatever the stalker had in mind for me."

"I was always very proud of him. As a little boy he always wanted to help everyone, and I can only imagine what sort of person he would have grown into if those crazy people hadn't taken him from me. But whilst I do appreciate you telling me all this, I don't really see how this is going to help me. You were right what you said back there, and for years I've searched for his body. I even wrote to his murderers in jail, pleading with them to tell me where his remains are. But it would seem they killed so many children, not even they remember where they put his remains. Zac's remains were the only ones never to be found."

"Well, I hope this is where I come in. Whilst leading me out of the woods, Zac told me that he was taken while playing and then killed. He said that you haven't been very well recently and can't rest until you lay him to rest properly. So, with your permission, I'd like to arrange for some people to escort us tonight back to the New Forest where your son can hopefully guide me to his resting place. Whilst I can't give you any guarantees that we will find them, I'm almost certain we can."

"Do you really think we can? I've waited for this for

years."

"Yes I really think we can," I say as I rise and give Margaret a cuddle.

"When do we leave?"

"Wait here while I get everything organised. I'll be back shortly."

"Penny you can't be serious about this. It's too dangerous, and the stalker is still out there. You know I support everything you do but this, this is just madness. You can't go back into the New Forest, not while the stalker is on the loose. Please don't do this; not yet, wait until Chris has found him at least."

"Russell, I know you're concerned but I have been reassured by Soul that I am safe tonight and I believe him. Now, there is a lady in there that needs to find the remains of her son; are you coming or not?"

"As if I'm going to let you out of my sight. Promise you will not leave my side."

"Oh, Russell, you are such a worrier. I'll try to stay by your side I promise. Now let's get going."

We have been driving along the various motorways that lead us back into the New Forest for the past few hours and eventually turn onto the A31. I begin to feel uneasy as I tell Russell to continue towards Brockenhurst. It's the first time I've been back here since the kidnapping and the feeling of unease settles in my stomach the closer we get. I ask for Soul's reassurance and strength as we approach the forestry area that I escaped from. Pulling into a layby not far from the place where I fell into Russell's arms, I take some much needed cleansing deep breaths before I exit the car. At the entrance to the forest I see my beautiful spirit friend patiently waiting for me.

Russell joins my side. "Stay close to me at all times, Penny. I don't like this one bit, but having said that I understand your reasons."

I nod at him in response and then close my eyes and focus my attention on my spirit friend as I tune into his energy. Chris approaches us with Margaret and we make our way towards the entrance of the forest.

"We need to enter here and follow the path round to the right."

We begin our journey into the forest and follow the makeshift path round to the right. As we venture further into the forest, the path begins to disappear and we find ourselves walking carefully over exposed tree roots and our route becomes increasingly narrow. Stopping at a fallen tree, we rest for a while so that Margaret can get her breath back. I tune into my spirit friend for reassurance that we are on the right path, thankful that we are heading in a slightly different direction to that in which the burnt down hut remains.

"Zac says there's not much further to go," I find myself telling everyone.

"He's here with us?"

"Yes, he is guiding us to his resting place. Do you think you're OK to continue?"

"I've waited so long to find him…please, I must try to keep going."

I stand and focus my attention again and proceed to lead the group deeper into the forest. The sky becomes dark as we lose daylight, but the glow of light surrounding my spirit friend lights the way ahead.

We move into a clearing at the edge of some water where my spirit friend moves towards an old oak tree, which is overhanging the water. My spirit friend turns to me and says, 'My remains are here beside this tree right next to the water.'

"Your son says his remains are beside this oak tree, the one overhanging the water."

We stand for a while and watch Chris tape off the area while we wait for a team of forensics to arrive.

"Margaret, maybe we should get you a place close by to stay while we wait for news; after all, it is late and getting cold, and it will probably take a few hours or maybe even the night for forensics to clear the area."

"No, I've waited a long time to find my son. I want to stay here."

Thankfully, Brett arrived with chairs and blankets to keep us all warm while forensics set up a white tent over the area and began to dig into the earth. We didn't have to wait too long before the news came from inside the tent to confirm that they had found the remains of a small child buried in a shallow grave by the tree. One of the forensic team come over to us and produced a rather mudded blue rag type shirt.

"Do you recognise this shirt Mrs…?"

"Mrs Meadows, but you can call me Margaret," she replied as her shaking hands reach for the shirt.

"I'm sorry, I can't let you touch the shirt just yet. I just need to know if you recognise it."

Nodding with tearful eyes she whispers, "That's my Zac's shirt."

===== X =====

Chapter Nineteen

As I kiss Russell goodbye this morning my stomach ties up in knots and I get a really strange feeling, a feeling that I can't quite describe.

"Be careful today, Russell."

"I'm always careful, just promise me that when you go to your art class today that Chris will be with you. I know we need to get things back to normal but that doesn't stop me worrying about you, and after yesterday's excursions, I don't want you overdoing things."

"I will, I promise. Look, oh I don't know it's probably nothing, but something doesn't feel right today, almost like something bad is going to happen but I'm not sure what."

"Make sure you keep Chris with you at all times and call me if you need me to come home. I love you, my beautiful lady, see you tonight."

"Love you too, handsome, stay safe."

As soon as Russell's car pulls away I turn to go inside and I'm overcome with a really strong sense of unease. Something is definitely wrong today. I just can't put my finger on it but maybe I should quiet my mind for a while before I go down to my art class. I close the front door and then hear buzzing in my ear, like someone is trying to get my attention. As I walk towards the kitchen, I suddenly get this sharp pain in my chest. *Russell*, I think to myself. Calling out to Chris I throw open the front door and run down the long driveway, following the direction of Russell's car. Something is going to happen to Russell. I must get him back to the house.

As I start to pull out of Penny's long driveway, I notice something in the road blocking my exit. I step out of the car and walk over to it when 'bang', there is a loud noise and my body is jolted backwards. "Russell," I can hear Penny running towards me as I place my hand on my chest and feel the blood oozing out of me. I try to tell her to go back to the house; it's not safe, but no words come out as I fall forwards towards the ground. *Penny, no go back*, I try to say as I pass out cold on the road in front of my car.

"Russell! No! Call an ambulance! Someone, please call an ambulance!"

Falling to my knees I cradle his face in my hands and the tears fall down my cheeks. "Don't you leave me, Russell. Stay with me...help is on its way."

Blood is pouring out of his chest and I try to apply pressure to the area while I wait for help to arrive.

I feel like I'm floating somewhere. I look down towards someone lying on the floor. Penny, she seems to be cradling someone on the floor. *What's going on? Why is Penny cradling someone?* I look down at the lifeless body on the floor and hear people rushing around with some kind of machine; one of them looks at me and then continues to do God knows what to the poor sod that's lying on the floor. *I don't want to be here*, I think to myself. *I shouldn't be here.*

"No, Russell, don't you leave me."

I hear Penny cry out and then after a loud bang, my life falls into darkness.

"He's back with us; we need to get him into surgery. Hurry, he's lost a lot of blood."

I have been sitting inside this blasted waiting room for hours, yet there is still no news. What the hell are they doing in there to him? Is he still alive? Just when I find someone who I care enough about to spend the rest of my life with, bam, just like that it feels like they are being taken away from me. As I get up to pace up and down again I wonder if it will be any use trying to find someone again to see if there is any news. Although I might scream at them, if one more person tells me that he is still in surgery, I swear I'm going to blow a fuse. Just as I turn to look at the door I can feel the presence of Soul enter the room. I'm really not in the mood for this right now, I think to myself.

'I know,' Soul whispers in my ear.

'Yeah right, I forgot for a minute there, you hear all of my thoughts.'

'I just come to let you know the surgery is going well. He is not out of the woods just yet but all is going well.'

'I appreciate you telling me this, Soul, but I really don't feel like company right now.'

'Penny, you know how this works; the more you need us, the closer we come.'

'No offence, but right now, I'm struggling to understand anything spiritual. If you are real, why would you have promised me that he was my soul mate and that we were meant to be together? Some crazy stalker has shot the only man that's ever really loved me for who I am and is lying in that theatre probable dying for all I know. So this is one of those times when I think I have every right to question my spiritual work, don't you think?

'Right now I feel like this is all just a figment of my imagination. That I'm making all this up and even seeing you standing there is just unreal. How come I can help other people yet I can't even help myself. Can you explain that to me? Well. Why didn't you tell me, Soul? Why wait until he was about to be shot to warn me of it. I just don't understand.'

'This is a part of Russell and your life plan; you know we can't interfere with a person's choice. We can only support it.'

'This just gets better; so he decided to get shot because of me.'

'I didn't say that; maybe it's to make you realise what you've got. Have you looked at it this way?'

Chris enters the room looking rather exhausted and interrupting any further conversation between Soul and myself.

"We got him. The guy's name is Robert Newton, and according to his neighbours, he's a real loner. He mostly keeps himself to himself according to the guy in the flat next to his. It would seem that he hears voices though, and shot Russell because someone in his head told him it was the only way to get Russell out of the way so that he could be with you. It would seem he is somewhat delusional, and believes that he has a life to make with you. When we searched his flat earlier, it was full of clippings and pictures of you, which would indicate that this guy is completely obsessed with you, Penny."

"Well, thank God you got him. Let's hope they lock him up and throw away the key for what he's done to poor Russell."

"I don't think he will be getting out anytime soon."

"Good."

'Look at me disappointed all you like, Soul. I'm not going to feel any compassion towards someone who just shot my man.'

I'm floating on a cloud somewhere, but I'm not quite sure where. It is quiet and peaceful all around me, yet in the distance I can hear voices. I'm not sure where they are coming from but I know one of the voices belongs to Penny. I'm sure I hear the sobs of my mother but they fade in the distance as I float and drift on and on in this peaceful place.

"He has been drifting in and out of consciousness for two days, Penny. Have the doctors not said when he will be back with us?"

"I'm not sure, Sylvia. Every time I ask them they just say because of the blood loss his body needs time to recover."

"You must know something; can't you use your spiritual magic to bring him back to us?"

"I'm afraid my spiritual magic as you put it is pretty useless at the moment."

"But you help so many people with your work. Why is it not helping?"

"I've been asking myself that same question over and

over. Rose is coming in later, so maybe she'll be able to help."

"I guess we just sit and wait then."

"I guess that's all we can do."

The cloud that I'm floating on suddenly drifts further upwards towards a bright light. Strange, although the light is bright, it doesn't seem to hurt my eyes. As the cloud I'm sitting on approaches a gate, I notice that the gate is open. But I'm feeling so tranquil floating on this cloud. I just want to sit and drift outside the gate, when the voices of Penny and Rose sound out to me.

"Penny, you can't give up on your spiritual work."

"Why not, it's not exactly doing anything to help me now is it?"

"Penny, of course it is. Soul and your guardian angels are here helping you through this."

"Where, I don't see anyone. I've tried the healing, it's not working, nothing is working...he is still lying here comatose and not responding."

"You are not thinking clearly, that's why you can't see them. Penny, you know how this works."

"Yeah, Soul told me a few days ago. Actually, I do feel a little guilty for being rude to him."

"He understands you're under a lot of pressure at the moment, what with the father of your unborn child lying in a hospital bed."

What? Penny is pregnant with my child? What am I doing here drifting on this cloud? I should be down there comforting her. But she said she couldn't have children, so how could this of happened. 'Well are you going to sit there all day floating and day dreaming? You are given a choice now and be grateful because very few people get this choice. You can either come through this gate with me your sister, or go back to the love of your life, so what's it gonna be, Russ.'

'Suzie, we miss you so much, but I don't understand

how you can be here, you're de—'

'Yes I know, pretty amazing isn't it. My body died but my soul lives on, Russ. I visit you every day.'

'But where am I, and what am I doing here? Am I dead too?'

'So many questions, Russ, you were shot right. Your body is alive but needs time to recover so your soul has travelled to the gate of heaven. I have been watching you for days, whether your body lives or dies is entirely up to you now.'

'It is so peaceful here, but Penny she is pregnant with my child. Will she ever marry me now?'

'There is only one way to find out, Russ. The decision is yours. I love you to by the way.'

'Love you too, little sis.'

I try to reach out to Penny but nothing moves and my hands feel glued to my side. Did I just dream that I saw Suzie or was it really true? It would have been wonderful to stay in that peaceful place with her but I have a lot of things I would like to do in the world that I'm familiar with.

Slowly I feel my eyes begin to open and see Penny has fallen asleep with her head resting at the side of my arm. I try to clear my throat. God, I could really use a drink right now.

"Russell.Oh, thank God. Let me get the nurse."

I try to speak but no words come out as my throat is so dry, so weakly, I point to the jug of water on the hospital table.

"Water, right, yes. Let me just check with the nurse."

The door to my room opens and a middle-aged nurse walks over to the bed. She checks my vitals and cheerily chats away to me as she does so. I'm too busy watching Penny to take much notice of what she's saying. There's only one question on my mind at this moment in time and it doesn't involve any nurse. Finally, the blasted woman leaves the room with a cheery exit.

Penny fills the glass on the table with water and places

a straw in it. She brings it over to me and I take a long soothing drink before facing the woman that I love, and clearing my throat again, I ask her the question that I've asked her before, but this time I want a different answer.

"Marry me?"

"Yes, Russell, I'll marry you."

"Was that a yes?"

"Hum and I think you're going to be a daddy."

"You're pregnant."

"Yes."

"But how?"

"Does it matter?"

"No, of course not. Blimey, I'm going to be a daddy and marry the most beautiful woman in the world. Penny, you've made me the happiest man alive. I can't believe it."

"Well, you better believe it because it's gonna happen as soon as you're well enough."

My God, I'm so glad I came back, I think to myself as I stare at the most beautiful woman I've ever met. Life just doesn't get much better than this.

Epilogue

Who would have thought that a few years ago I would have married again and given birth to a healthy baby boy? As I sit on the picnic rug at Coltishaw and watch father and son play happily, I think back to our wedding day. White sands, blue sea, sun in the sky and the best thing was the look on my husband's face as I walked bare foot on the sand towards him. Me with my purple and cream dress and him with his cream trousers rolled up at the bottom. Yeah, well it wasn't your normal traditional wedding but it was exactly what we both wanted. Eloping, well not exactly, the most important people we needed there came with us to the Bahamas and we married on the most beautiful beach you could ever imagine. The sound of the waves as we exchanged our own personal written vows underneath an archway of flowers...it was just beautiful.

There's not a day that hasn't gone by since I revealed my past to Russell that he hasn't told me how beautiful I am. Every time he comes close to me he whispers, "I love you, beautiful." I can't believe how lucky I was to find him. Who would have thought that I would meet the man of my dreams at one of my shows? The minute our eyes connected I knew there was something between us, but looking back to how I felt then, I was sworn off men for life and he had a fiancé. How time and situations have a way of changing the way we see things.

Now I look at the two most important men in my life and can't believe how lucky I am. I wouldn't change a thing. Maybe I'll announce my little surprise to them both when they come back over, I think to myself as the ice cream van plays his music.

"Mummy, Mummy, Daddy said I can have an ice cream. Do you want one?" my son shouts as he rushes over to me.

"Sure thing. Let's go catch Daddy up before he eats it

all himself."

I pick Johnathan up in my arms and swing him around in the air. We rush together over to Russell, who is waiting in line.

"What can I get for my two favourite people?" Russell asks

"I think we'll have a ninety-nine. What do you reckon, Johnathan?"

"Yeah."

We take our ice-creams over to the picnic rug and munch away on them. I smile to myself as I think about everything we've been through together and know that despite the past, the stalker and the awful shooting, nothing will ever tear us apart.

"Why are you smiling? You're up to something I can tell."

"I'm not up to anything," I play innocently.

"Come on, my beautiful lady, out with it."

"Well how would you like to be a Daddy again?"

"You're pregnant!"

"Yes."

"Oh, Penny, that is just the best news. A brother or sister for Johnathan then our family will be complete. I love you so much, my beautiful lady."

"I love you too, handsome man of mine."

===== **X** =====

I would like to take this opportunity to thank all you readers for taking the time to read my story. Remember, when you look in the mirror see yourself through the eyes of your guardian angel, beautiful and magical just by being who you truly are.

Acknowledgements

I wish to thank everybody at New Generation Publishing for all their help and support in bringing this book to publication, with special thanks to David and Sam for all their help and reassurance along the way. I would also like to give a huge thank you to my Mum Janet and best friends Irene and Meena, for their constant support and encouragement during the writing of this book. Thanks also to my husband and children who have allowed me the time and space to write. I give much thanks and gratitude to my Dad, guides and loved ones, who I'm sure have helped me along the way from the spiritual realms. God Bless to you all.

Lightning Source UK Ltd.
Milton Keynes UK
UKOW02f0613160916

283125UK00002B/8/P